Prelude and Promises

By Author Barbara Baldwin

Print ISBNs
Amazon Print 978-0-2286-0562-1
B&N Print 978-0-2286-0563-8

BWL Publishing Inc.

Books we love to write ...
Authors around the world.

http://bwlpublishing.ca

Dedication

To the real Brenda Kay-- A special friend in my life.

A Few Musical Terms

Adagio—Restful, at ease. A slow moving tempo.

Capriccio—A quick, improvisational, spirited piece of music.

Concerto—A composition written for a solo instrument, such as the piano.

The orchestra plays the accompaniment while the soloist plays the melody.

Counterpoint—Two or three melodic lines played at the same time.

Legato—Indicates the entire composition, or the movement, is to be played smoothly.

Presto—Indicates the tempo of the music is to be very fast.

Sonata—A musical piece consisting of four movements, each differing in tempo, rhythm
and melody but held together by subject and style.

Chapter 1

Cheyenne stepped onto the boardwalk outside the Bed & Breakfast and slipped on her sunglasses to cut the glare of the late morning light. The only redemption from the hot July sun was the breeze blowing off the nearby bay. She sighed. She wasn't here to enjoy the pristine beach and crystal blue water of the small tourist town. She was on a mission and today she would run her quarry to ground, if she had to burn down every tavern in a two mile radius.

For days, he had managed to evade her. His minions in the little village of Princetown refused to give him up. The first day, the answer to her question as to where Joseph Donovan was had been met with "Who?" as though no one in the town of a few hundred people had ever even heard of the man.

Yesterday, it seemed everyone in town had agreed to send her on the wildest goose chase ever to be had. One comment from a local led to another place where, of course, the next person sent her off in a different direction. She knew, that they knew, where he lived, but no one gave her a residence. They simply pointed her to yet another business, most of which were bars.

They apparently thought she was after him for nefarious reasons, which for the love of God was ridiculous. Did they think she had no sense at all that she would waste her time in some backwater village, dumping sand out of her shoes every day, in pursuit of some…some male who had made it his recent goal to negate obligations and run away from his responsibilities? No, this was strictly business.

If only her employer had not insisted *she* be the one to find him…

Two months earlier at the Donovan Academy of Music in Chicago, Illinois

"You will find my nephew," Sebastian Everhart Donovan had told her in no uncertain terms.

"Sir, he's thirty years old. He has a right—"

"He has a gift, and that gift is meant to be shared. He belongs to the world."

"Why not hire a private investigator? Surely they have skills I don't."

"And make this public?" He quickly interrupted her. "I'll not have the tabloids spewing vindictive lies about him being on drugs, cavorting with seamy actresses and singers or doing God knows what. You have three months."

"Sir, I doubt I can—"

"Three months, Miss Tucker. Because that is all the time I have." He bent his head to the papers on his desk, effectively dismissing her.

She knew he had been ill, but now as she looked closer, she noticed the pallor of his skin and how his suit jacket seemed to sag on his shoulders. His hand shook as he tried to pick up a pen and if she weren't mistaken, his hair was thinning; almost bald on top.

"Sir, is there anything I can do?"

"You can do as you're told," he grumbled, but most of the starch normally in his voice was gone. "And you will say nothing to my nephew other than he needs to return to his rightful place."

That rightful place was as a world renowned pianist. Joseph Everhart Donovan had been groomed by his uncle for his role from the age of six. Having worked for the Uncle for the past six years, Cheyenne knew only some of his story. His mother had been a concert violinist, raised by her brother, a great composer. She had disappeared for a time at age twenty and come home unmarried but pregnant. After Joseph's birth, no one had heard anything more about Kathryn Donovan. She hadn't performed in years and had become a complete recluse yet no one in the media had ever speculated why. And believe it; Cheyenne had done plenty of research on the family after she had come to work for the Donovan Academy of Music. Because even though she lived on the Donovan premises, in all her years as Mr. Donovan's executive assistant, she had never seen his sister.

She hadn't even known Kathryn Donovan had died until one of the servants let it slip that *Master* Donovan had left in a temper immediately after the funeral and no one had seen him since. That had been two weeks ago.

She sighed as she quietly closed the door to Mr. Donovan's office. What did she know about finding missing people?

The easiest place to start her search did not prove the most helpful. She spent a month going through company records, looking for some hint as to where he might have gone; some trip he may have taken that didn't correspond to a performance. Then she started in on the financial accounts. Although his uncle maintained power over the trust that funded the Academy, Joseph had access to funds at will. Having pinched pennies her entire life, Cheyenne was well aware of the value of a dollar, and it didn't take long for her to recognize a pattern.

She brought the matter to the attention of Mr. Donovan. "Joseph made systematic withdrawals every month for over a year."

He did not seem surprised. "Joseph has access to the trust, within reason, although all performance expenses and travel are usually handled through the accountant."

"These are cash withdrawals; a thousand every two weeks." An extreme amount of money from Cheyenne's perspective.

The man just shrugged, not looking up from his papers. "He may have had a mistress. I don't pry into his personal affairs, as long as he's discrete and leaves nothing behind that requires responsibility."

7

She blushed at the intimate statement, having an idea to what he referred, but that wasn't her concern. "That's a rather large sum of money."

Again he shrugged. "It was cash. There's no way of tracing it. Are there no receipts for airline tickets; hotel rooms?"

"Nothing outside his performance agenda."

"Then keep looking."

"Another question, if I may, sir?"

With a resigned sigh, he set aside his pen, folded his hands on the paper in front of him and regarded her with limp, watery eyes. He really did not look well.

"Do you know who his friends are; college pals or other close musicians?"

"You do not have friends when you are famous," the uncle stated flatly. "You have business associates and groupies; and those who would take advantage of you." His tone was bitter.

She replied before she thought better of it. "That doesn't seem a very happy way to live."

He skewered her with a look. "Your plebeian outlook does not interest me."

His comment about the lack of friends bothered her more than it should have. Everyone should have friends; someone to confide in. Her best friend was her younger sister, whom she still called twice a week even though she didn't see her often.

The conversation with Mr. Donovan triggered a memory of an incident that had occurred, what, six months ago?

Her office and Mr. Donovan's private teaching studio were connected to the mansion by a covered walkway over the driveway. Joseph, his mother and his uncle all lived in the main house. Her apartment was behind her office, and she rarely had reason to visit the mansion. On the occasions she had meals with the servants, she used the back entrance which led directly to the kitchen.

On this particular day, she had papers Mr. Donovan needed to sign but he had left early, not indicating whether

8

he would be back. Since the papers were time sensitive, she hurried after him, hoping to catch him before it was too late.

Instead, she ran into Joseph, literally, in the foyer. He managed to catch her before she sprawled on the marble floor, but in doing so he dropped his briefcase and the contents spilled out. She squatted to help him gather a pile of mail.

"That's not necessary," he had said as he quickly grabbed the stack from her. "A friend. I'm collecting his mail for him."

She caught only a glimpse of an envelope from a Travel company. "Well, he must be taking a trip." She handed him the envelope but at the time had wondered at the flush on his face.

Now, as she recalled the incident, she thought perhaps finding his friend would lead her to Joseph. The problem was she hadn't paid much attention to the recipient's name on the envelope. She had just noticed the business name. What had it been?

It wasn't until the next day that Cheyenne remembered the company name, but an internet search came up with dozens of possibilities for Island Realty and Travel. She started calling but no one had heard of Joseph Donovan, at least not in regard to that name and purchasing real estate in their area. The last on her list, a company in Lockabee, Washington, gave her the first sense of a lead, and that came only from a *lack* of helpfulness.

"I know Joseph Donovan. I love his music," said the woman on the other end of the line.

"Yes, but have you recently rented or sold any real estate to him, or perhaps to a friend with whom he is traveling?"

The woman hesitated just long enough for Cheyenne to get the sense she was withholding information. "Our records are confidential."

"Nonsense. Selling houses is on public record."

"Then perhaps you should start there." And the phone disconnected.

It was all Cheyenne needed. She booked a ticket to Seattle and flew out the next day.

Now, she stood on the boardwalk in the small village of Princetown on Lockabee Island off the coast of Washington state. Hands on hips, she looked first one way then the other. It was approaching noon, and for a young man who had grown up with servants, she could assume that he didn't cook and would be eating lunch at some local restaurant. Today she wouldn't ask questions; that had gotten her nowhere. She would simply look.

It didn't take long to realize that most of the restaurants in the area were occupied by tourists – middle aged couples or families. She narrowed her search to taverns, of which there seemed to be plenty. Number four, the Gold Pelican, was as dim inside as the rest. She stood by the door and removed her sunglasses to let her eyes adjust, surveying the occupants. Several tables were empty by this time. A couple of men dressed in black eyed her from the end of the bar, but she ignored them.

She approached the bartender, one of the same men who had sent her chasing around town yesterday.

"You again? I told you yesterday I don't know Joseph Donovan except for my girl friend dragging me to a concert in Seattle once." He shrugged. "I guess it wasn't bad."

"Wasn't bad?" Cheyenne sputtered. "He is world-renowned; the finest pianist to ever perform."

The bartender wasn't impressed. "Want a drink?"

Frustrated, Cheyenne nodded. "Lemonade?"

When the bartender came back with her drink, she slid a twenty across the bar. "Perhaps Joseph Donovan was here with a friend. You've been here for some time, I'm sure. You must notice non-residents."

He eyed the bill but she kept her fingers securely on top of it.

"I rarely pay attention to the tourists, unless they get rowdy."

Patience, Cheyenne muttered to herself.

"Not a tourist but not a life-time resident. Someone who has been here, say, about two months."

"No one by the name of Joe."

Cheyenne racked her brain for the name on the envelope he had dropped that day, which she had only seen upside-down. Jeremy…John…Jake!

""I'm looking for Jake."

"Jake who?"

Now what? How many Jakes could there be in a town this size?

"Well, you see. That's the thing." She glanced down, trying for a shy look. "We met at a…concert, and we didn't exactly get around to last names."

The man laughed, seeming to understand all she hadn't said. "That sounds like Jake." He looked closer. "You don't exactly look his type, but if he wanted you to find him, wouldn't he have given you his last name or a number?"

She bit her lip. She never lied and it wasn't easy. "We had been drinking, and…"

"Hit and run, did he?" the man said and though she had no idea what exactly that meant, she nodded.

"Hmm, it might be kind of interesting to see what Jake does when you show up." He turned to a phone on the counter and punched in a few numbers, his back to her.

Lord, how backward was this place when people still had land lines?

In minutes he hung up. "Jake said have a beer and he'd be here in a few."

"I don't want a beer." Her stomach had begun somersaulting and her hand shook slightly as she lifted her glass for a swallow of lemonade. After two long months, did she dare hope this Jake could tell her where Joseph was?

"Excuse me, miss," one of the men in black slid down the bar closer to where she sat. "Did you mention Joseph Donovan?"

She started to answer but paused. Mr. Donovan had always cautioned her about gossip and apparently this man had overheard her.

"Do you know him?" she asked cautiously.

11

The man looked at his companion before answering. "In college. Haven't seen him in years so when you mentioned his name…"

Cheyenne narrowed her gaze. The man looked to be well over forty, not exactly close to Joseph's age. And she knew Joseph had had a private education. Something about the man made her wary.

"I haven't seen him," she said, which wasn't a lie. She turned her back and after a few minutes, heard the man shuffle down to the end of the bar.

She kept her eye on the door, not sure who she was looking for when a group of men walked in. One in particular drew her attention. His sun bleached hair was shaggy and long; he wore an untucked polo shirt and stained cargo shorts, his long legs and forearms tan. Although he looked nothing like Joseph, something about his posture, even relaxed as he chatted with the men who came in with him, reminded her of times when she had seen him off stage after a performance.

When his gaze collided with hers, his eyes narrowed and he frowned. She thought he intended to run as he turned back to his companions, but after a few brief words, he left them and headed her way, sliding onto a stool to her right.

"Well, well, if it isn't Miss Tucker. I wondered how long it would take my uncle to send someone after me. I never thought he would use you."

She recognized his voice if not his appearance. All traces of the meticulous performer were gone.

"Joseph! Oh my god, I can't believe I finally found you."

"Joseph?" the bartender echoed, setting a beer in front of him. "This is Jake; the guy you said screwed you and ran off."

Joseph raised a brow and frowned at her and she had the grace to blush. Ignoring the bartender, she turned to face him.

"Your uncle didn't *use* me. He asked for my help."

Joseph's voice held anger. "You have no idea how devious my uncle can be. Sending a guy to manhandle me wouldn't have accomplished his purpose as easily as sending a beautiful woman to seduce me."

"I most certainly did not come to seduce you." Even as she spoke, she felt the heat of a blush at his compliment.

"I thought I had hidden my tracks very well and yet you found me." He looked her up and down and Cheyenne fought the urge to tug her skirt down.

She cleared her throat, determined to get to the business at hand. Instead, she asked curiously, "Why did the bartender call you Jake?"

"It's my name," he said before taking a swallow of beer.

She frowned because she knew better, however there seemed little sense in arguing. In a low voice, she said, "I can understand why you would use a fake name. Every time I asked after Joseph Donovan, everyone had heard *of* you, but no one knew where you were."

He seemed amused at her words. She cleared her throat and straightened her shoulders. "Now that we have that cleared up, I have a message from Mr. Donovan."

He put up a finger. "Hold that thought. Would you excuse me for a minute? Then we'll go somewhere and talk."

Cheyenne watched him saunter between tables toward the facilities at the back of the bar. One of the two men who had spoken to her earlier also left his perch and disappeared into the back.

Cheyenne finished her lemonade and waited. The man returned, shook his head at his companion and they both walked past her and left. She looked to the rear hallway once more and frowned.

Ten minutes later she knew she had been taken in by the oldest trick in the book; one she had even used on a blind date.

Chapter 2

Cheyenne hurried out of the bar, looking both ways but could find no one wearing a blue polo hurrying away.

"Quick," she said as she flagged down a bicycle taxi, climbing onto the small rickshaw seat. "I'm looking for a man who just left that bar."

"Honey aren't we all," replied the girl as she swung her leg over the seat and began pedaling. "What's he look like?" she called over her shoulder.

Not even thinking, she said, "It's Joseph Donovan."

Cheyenne grabbed the side handle to keep from tumbling out as the girl slammed on the brakes.

"What?" She turned on the seat to stare at her. "*He's* here on the island? I love his music. I love *him*! What a hunk."

Cheyenne shook her head. She was beginning to understand why Joseph wasn't using his real name. "Blue polo and cargo shorts; shaggy blonde streaked hair."

The girl scrunched her brow. "That doesn't sound like Joseph Donovan. I saw him in concert last year and he was—"

"Yes, yes, I know. Maybe it wasn't him. Can we just go? You drive; I'll look."

An hour later after riding up and down all the back streets and narrow alleys of the small town, Cheyenne gave the taxi driver all the cash she had in her purse when she dropped her off at the Bed & Breakfast.

"You owe me another twenty dollars."

Cheyenne had to admire her entrepreneurial spirit; getting paid to exercise all day. "That's all the cash I have.

I'll have to find an ATM." She handed the girl her business card. "If you'll trust me, come back in the morning and I'll hire you for the day."

"Deal." The girl stuck out her hand. "I'm Lindsay, by the way. Here's my card with my number. I'm independent so you can't request me from any of the regular taxi services."

Definitely a woman after her own heart, Cheyenne thought, as she stood on the boardwalk and watched Lindsay pedal away. Not the exercise part, she silently laughed as she went up the steps. She had wondered how she would get around when the port authority in Red Haven told her she couldn't drive her car onto the island. Apparently only residents could own vehicles, and from what she had seen, they were all small, antiquated cars with rust around the wheel wells and license plates held on with wire. Tourists relied on bicycle rentals or the rickshaw bicycle taxis for hire. Since she had never learned to ride a bike, she had been walking or taking a taxi.

Speaking of walking, she doubted she could do any more today. She dropped into the brocade chair in her room and removed her shoes, rubbing the soles of her feet. She hadn't expected to spend more than a day; three at the most, finding Joseph and had not packed quite right. She stared at the four inch heels now tossed carelessly on the carpet. The red patent exactly matched her purse and the pinstripe in her suit. It was one of her favorite work outfits, but she had chosen it for sitting professionally at a desk and walking in air conditioned comfort, not trudging around in the heat on wooden sidewalks.

Her stomach growled, reminding her how long ago breakfast had been. She reached down for her shoes and her feet automatically tucked under as though they had minds of their own. The thought of putting her shoes back on, much less walking very far in them, was just not an option. She had a pair of low heels, but they were meant for trousers. Her stomach rumbled louder. There was no help for it. She would have to change her clothes in order to eat.

Damn Joseph Donovan anyway. This was all his fault, and when she caught up with him, she would certainly give him a piece of her mind.

The street in front of the Inn was bustling with tourists and normally Cheyenne would have enjoyed people watching. Tonight the bumping and jostling irritated her. One more thing to lie at Donovan's door. She stopped at the closest restaurant and managed to get a seat at the bar since apparently the tables were reserved for groups of more than one. Unfortunately a single woman sitting at a bar, even if it was in a restaurant, invited unwanted company. Between her salad and main course, she had to deflect the advances of three different men.

Her list of grievances just kept growing.

Upon finishing her meal, she inquired as to the location of the nearest ATM, and was heading back to the Inn when her cell rang. It was after ten; too late for her sister to be calling unless there was an emergency. Cheyenne's hand shook as she dug through her purse, but when she looked at the readout, it was an unidentified number.

She dropped the phone into her purse and finished her walk back to her room. She never answered numbers not in her contact list. If it was someone who needed to get in touch, they would leave a voice mail. If not, it wasn't important.

Mrs. Godfrey, the owner of the Bed & Breakfast, usually left out wine and tea for the evening and Cheyenne poured a glass of Merlot to take upstairs to her room. It wasn't until she plugged in her phone to charge that she noticed the voice mail light blinking.

"So, unknown contact, are you someone wanting to extend the warranty on the car I don't own, or a scammer wanting my credit card number?" she muttered as she punched play.

"Miss Tucker, this is Jake Smith," a deep voice rumbled over the line.

"I don't know any Jake Smith." Cheyenne started to jab the delete button but paused. "Jake?" Her jabbering made her miss part of his message. She quickly hit repeat.

"Miss Tucker, this is Jake Smith." There was a pause and a heavy sigh before he continued. "I sincerely apologize for running out on you today. You caught me by surprise, but I hope you will let me make it up to you. I live out at Crystal Bay if you would come out tomorrow so we can talk." Another pause, then a short, "Please," before a click ended the message.

She smiled. Tomorrow was certainly looking up.

* * *

The morning dawned clear with the promise of hot, but Cheyenne dressed in her best suit and heels. If she was to convince Joseph to return to Chicago, she needed all the confidence her professional attire gave her. She called Lindsay as she went down to breakfast, and the rickshaw was waiting when she exited the Inn.

"Do you know where Crystal Bay is?" she asked as she climbed onto the seat.

"There's no place on the island I don't know, but that's not a much inhabited area. Are you sure that's where you want to go?" Even as she asked, she started pedaling down the narrow street.

"That's the name he...my client gave me."

Lindsay grinned over her shoulder. "That's definitely a very nice, isolated spot to meet a...client."

Cheyenne's look of distain was lost on the girl. She certainly had no designs on this particular *client.* As they flew along what appeared to be the only road out of town, she thought about what she knew of Joseph Donovan. Her job was executive assistant to Mr. Sebastian Donovan, who was a composer in his own right but also gave private music lessons and ran a music academy in downtown Chicago. She had rarely seen Joseph as he was constantly on tour and had his own staff but when she had, he had been reserved and aloof. She knew the trust money that ran the Academy had come from Joseph's winning the coveted Camelot Award for Excellence in Musical Composition when he was just eighteen, then again two years ago at the age of twenty-eight. He had a distinguished recording career and his concerts were sold out months in advance. Yet all that was the public Joseph Donovan, adored by millions and worth billions. She realized she didn't know the man behind the tuxedo at all.

"This is about the only cottage along this side of the island," Lindsay said as she came to a halt in front of a ramshackle structure that Cheyenne was sure a strong wind would blow out to sea. The porch sloped to one side and the shutters, faded to the palest blue, hung by one hinge or were missing altogether. Weeds had overtaken any flowers that may once have graced the front yard.

She warily climbed the steps and knocked on the door but no one answered.

"Want me to hang around?" Lindsay was swigging a bottle of water and Cheyenne wished she had thought to provision herself. A noise caught her attention and she carefully picked her way to the side of the cottage. Down a grassy knoll, a dock projected out into the water. A man, whom she presumed was Donovan, sat in a boat tied to the dock.

"You really should get some different shoes," Lindsay called as Cheyenne stumbled on loose gravel. She caught herself, straightened and adjusted her suit jacket. One didn't approach a famous icon and expect to be heard in flip flops and cut offs.

"Thank you for your assistance getting here," she said drily. "I'll call you when I'm ready to return."

The girl grinned, eyeing her over the top of her sunglasses. "Right. I'll just keep a tab."

"That's not a very wise way to do business," Cheyenne started, but Lindsay had already turned around and was heading back to the road.

Gingerly she picked her way over the grass to the edge of a dock. She eyed it guardedly and tested its sturdiness with one foot.

18

"It'll hold you," he called.

"I'm not worried about that." She still hesitated, then carefully stepped on the first plank, making sure her heels were on the wood and not the spaces between.

"Thanks for coming." He continued his work without looking up.

"How did you know my phone number?"

"I've always had your number." He did look up then, cocked a brow and grinned at her.

"I sincerely doubt that." She straightened her shoulders, determined to get right to the business at hand.

"I…" It suddenly dawned on her what he was doing. "Dear god, your hands!"

He held up his hands, greasy from working on the motor. "Yeah, I'm a mess."

"You can't be doing that!" Even as she spoke, he turned a wrench the wrong way and his hand slammed against the motor cover.

"Son of a bitch." He shook it off and repositioned the wrench.

"Stop! Good Lord, are you crazy?" His hands were insured by Lloyd's of London and here he was playing mechanic.

He did stop. Hoisting himself onto the dock, he spun to face her.

"Exactly why are you here, Miss Tucker?" Although the question was asked with no intonation, she had the feeling he was judging her. She carefully chose her next words.

"You need to return to Chicago. You've had your little holiday and the staff is waiting to set the dates for the next concert season."

"There won't be a next season." He wasn't looking at her now, but was busily wiping grease from his hands on an equally dirty rag.

"You have a responsibility." Her voice rose with determination.

"To who? My uncle? As though he has ever done anything but take. His name on the Academy? He gave nothing but his name to that endeavor. He wasn't even at the dedication."

"You owe it to your audiences; to everyone who has ever bought an album or downloaded a single or gone to a concert. To all those taking piano lessons so they can be like you."

"I don't want anyone to be like me!" He threw the rag down on the dock and stood towering over her. "No one should be like me!"

She had had enough. He was still the arrogant, egotistical yet brilliant man she had first met six years ago. They would both have to cool down before he would see reason. She turned on her heel and started to storm away just as he yelled.

It was too late.

Her heels tangled in a rope on the dock and she went plunging into the water, only to surface to deep, male laughter.

"You, you maniac!" she screeched, struggling to her feet. The water was only three feet deep but she had gone completely under. Her hair dripped in her eyes and she swore she felt something creeping up her leg. She splashed to the dock and slapped her hands onto the wood to pull herself up but had no leverage.

"You could offer your assistance." She glared up at him.

He knelt before her, strong brown hands spread across his thighs. And he was still laughing. She couldn't recall hearing him laugh before. He had always been somber and studious. Laughter turned him even more handsome; his eyes twinkling, and his even white teeth gleaming in the sunlight. In that moment she both loathed him and ached for him.

"Forget it." She turned and tried to wade toward the shore but her heels, somehow still attached to her feet, sank into the sand. She floundered, her footing threatening to drag her down when she was grabbed beneath the arms and bodily lifted out of the water. Wobbling on the wooden planks, she grabbed his shoulders to keep herself upright.

"Crap," he muttered. Moving his hands down her leg, he lifted one foot then the other and yanked off her heels, unceremoniously throwing them back into the water.

She was beyond speech; almost. "Those are very, very expensive shoes!"

"Were. And probably the most stupid excuse for footwear ever created."

She stood there, barefoot and dripping wet, watching as his gaze slid down the sodden lines of her linen suit. His eyes lit and a slow smile curved his lips. He reached for her jacket buttons.

She felt her eyes widen and quickly stepped back, only to have him grab her arms to keep her from dropping back into the water.

"Don't even think it." She slapped at his hands.

"Seaweed," he said, holding up a piece of green slime he had plucked off her jacket. "Are you intent on drowning yourself rather than telling my uncle you couldn't persuade me to go home?"

His uncle was the absolute last person she was thinking about. Instead she was wondering how those slender fingers would feel against her wet skin and that would never do. She shivered at the thought.

He sighed and shook his head, moving past her to the edge of the dock. She watched him turn and tilt his head. "Come along, Miss Tucker. We can't send you back to my uncle all wet and wrinkled."

She had no recourse except to follow him up the grassy slope to the back deck.

Given the dilapidated outside of the cottage, Cheyenne was surprised when she stepped inside. The furniture was old and a little faded but everything was clean and neat. Several bright throw pillows added color to the brown couch. There was a small table and two chairs positioned between that and the efficiency kitchen. Most of the walls were simply banks of windows which gave it the appearance of living outside. She didn't understand how Joseph could live in such small confines, let alone making do for himself, when he came from such an entitled background.

He disappeared through a door and returned, tossing clothes at her. "The bathroom is the door on the right. Help yourself while I make some coffee."

She was shivering too much to come up with a retort to his curtness. The hot water felt good as she stood under the spray, but when she recalled that only a thin, unlocked door stood between them, she hurriedly finished and briskly rubbed her hair dry. Only when she reached for the clothes he had given her did she realize what they were – a faded pair of sweatpants and a ratty tee-shirt with a huge fish printed on the front.

An unbidden memory of her childhood with hand-me-down clothes she was often lucky to have surfaced and she quickly squelched it. She had worn nothing but designer suits, tailored pants and cashmere sweaters since her first paycheck. And yet she had no choice at the moment if she didn't want to wear the extra large bath towel which now covered her.

Jake watched Cheyenne emerge from the bathroom and his heart stopped. Gone was the prickly, straight laced Miss Tucker and in her place was a woman. His sweats were too large for her shapely hips and his tee shirt too small for her generous bust. The bass across the front looked entirely too happy. Her hair had begun curling around her shoulders and he wondered why she always wore it tightly up in some matronly bun. But it was her face, devoid of makeup, that drew him closer. She was beautiful; long lashes blinking over bright blue eyes; just a touch of natural color across her cheeks.

"You look...clean," he finished lamely, not sure exactly how to approach this new, totally different version of his uncle's executive assistant. He had rarely thought of her back in Chicago; she had simply been his uncle's efficient employee. Now, she stood looking hesitant and vulnerable, and he had the insane desire to pull her close and hug her.

She looked down, and he followed her gaze to see her curl her brightly painted toes. It would appear Miss Tucker had a sexy side. Those toes made him want to do something more than give her a brotherly hug. He cleared his throat. For all his sophistication on stage, in private he never knew exactly how to behave around people; especially women.

He relaxed as she said, "Are you using the name Jake Smith to appear incognito?"

"That's my real name." At her quizzical expression, he added, "A long story for another time. Lunch is ready." He turned back to the oven and pulled out the metal pan he had put in to bake before going to the dock.

"You cook?" She raised a brow in question.

"I used to sneak into the kitchen and watch Mrs. Miller." He shrugged. "I never had the chance to actually do it. I've found I enjoy it."

"I really should go back to town."

"Your clothes aren't dry. The least I can do is feed you." He turned back from taking two plates from the cupboard. "Besides, you don't have a ride."

"I can call Lindsay. She said she would come back when I was ready. I didn't think it would take long to explain why I was here."

"The explanation didn't take long." He grinned. "It was the arguing when I refused and you falling in the water that's extended your stay." When she opened her mouth to speak, he held up a hand. "Do not even attempt to blame that on me."

"And you shouldn't attempt to know what I'm thinking," she retorted, hands on hips.

His grin turned to a laugh. He liked this feisty version of Miss Tucker. "Touché." He pulled out a chair and waved her to it. "Sit."

Instead, she moved to the small kitchen. "I should help. You don't have to wait on me."

Her words were quiet and hesitant and when he glanced her way, she would not meet his gaze.

It took Jake a minute or two to realize the problem. "You are not on duty, Cheyenne." He deliberately used her

23

given name to cut through the formality. "You're just a woman and I'm just a guy." *Who wants to ask you out on a real date,* the thought popped unbidden into his head and from her look he was extremely glad he hadn't spoken aloud.

"There is nothing 'just a guy' about you," she said, but she did sit at the table so he proceeded to bring out lunch. "And that brings us back to the reason I am here."

He shook his head, pushing her plate toward her. "Food first. I for one know I'll need the stamina for my defense."

She looked down at her plate and he swore she blanched the color of a sheet. Using only her index finger and obviously not wanting to touch anything, she pushed it away.

"Are you allergic to cheese?" he asked. "Or gluten?"

She pinched her lips and shook her head.

"Then what?"

"I don't eat macaroni and cheese."

He raised a brow. "Ever?"

"Never."

Who didn't like Mac and cheese?

"You have to try it. This isn't the box variety. This is Mrs. Miller's special recipe which includes a healthy portion of cream cheese and three varieties of hard cheese."

From her expression, she wasn't impressed. He changed tact. "Let me put it another way. Unless you try my culinary efforts, I will not even think about your reason for being here."

Her shoulders slumped in defeat. "Why can't you simply go back to Chicago and see what your uncle wants. It may be totally innocuous."

"Because Uncle Sebastian never does anything without ulterior motives. So if he sent you, he wants something."

"Yes. He wants you back in Chicago."

He pushed her plate closer and raised a brow.

She gave him a disdainful look that in most cases would have caused Jake to back off, knowing his attention wasn't reciprocated. In this case, it only made him more determined. He wasn't at all sure why she interested him because she certainly wasn't his usual type of female. Perhaps that was the reason.

He poured them each some wine and started eating, watching her out of the corner of his eye but not saying a word. She finally poked a single macaroni with her fork and lifted it to her lips. He wondered what she had against macaroni and cheese. Given her taste in clothes, she probably thought it beneath her.

She nibbled cautiously then her eyes opened in surprise and she licked her lips before taking a full forkful. She ate over half of what he had put on her plate before pausing to sip her wine.

"There. Now you will please answer my question."

"Which question?"

"Why did you say what you did on the dock; that no one should be like you?"

He put down his fork with a sigh. She had kept her part of the bargain so it was only fair that he do the same.

"You have no doubt heard about the worldwide competition called the Camelot." At her nod, he continued. "The prize is a million dollars." He watched her eyes widen, "Exactly. This is the year of the competition and I can promise you it is why Uncle wants me back."

"You are gifted. Why wouldn't you want to try and win such a prestigious award?"

"I already have; at eighteen, and again at twenty-eight. That is what funds the Academy and all my uncle's endeavors. I simply have no desire, or need, to try it again."

While he had been talking she had finished off her Mac and cheese.

"Is that why you left? You didn't want to enter the competition," she asked.

He put another scoop of pasta on her plate before answering. "That doesn't even begin to touch on the problem. The music that once lightened my heart and fed my spirit has become a business; a profit and loss statement for my uncle. If I play 'x' number of performances a year for 'y' number of patrons, it would amount to 'z' income, minus the 'a' and 'b' of expenses and overhead."

She looked confused.

"I don't expect you to understand."

"I understand," she said as she got up and took her plate to the sink. "You have a gift you don't want to use. I would like to mention that the majority of people in this world would not only envy you the gift but the money it allowed you to obtain."

In a sense she was right, but he had come to the point in his life where he wanted to be an average, normal guy, responsible only for himself. He wanted to go out on a date without being recognized and interrupted. He wanted friends who liked him because he knew dirty jokes. He had found some of what he searched for here on Lockabee and he wasn't ready to give it up.

"I'll take you back to town now."

Without a word, she went and gathered her clothes from the bath, emerging with them bundled in her arms. But he should have known she wasn't going to give up.

"You must realize I'll be back tomorrow. This conversation is not over."

He grinned. "Would you like to spend the night to save the trouble of returning in the morning?" In their very short acquaintance, Jake now found the irresistible urge to tease the very proper and professional Miss Tucker. As predicted, she sputtered as she stomped past him.

"In your dreams!"

He held the door open for her, bowed at the waist and lifted his arm in a sweeping flourish. *I can only hope,* he murmured.

Chapter 3

Cheyenne remained quiet for the few minutes it took Joseph to drive her to town. She thought about his comments and how for some, the grass seem greener on the other side. Their conversation had allowed her a glimpse of the man inside the performer; a man who caused a tendril of desire to surface. At that point, she was glad he had offered to take her back to town. The small cottage was too intimate.

She turned slightly to observe him. His arms were brown from the sun, the muscles well defined as he gripped the steering wheel with hands that were rough and calloused, with a band-aid across two knuckles. His face, with its classic brows and nose and high cheek bones, should have been enough beauty for any one man, but no. Intense brown eyes drew you in, and God forbid if he smiled. His lips curved in the kind of sensual enticement no woman could resist.

Cheyenne turned back to the window. She had noticed all this, of course, when she first came to work for Mr. Donovan; she would have to be dead not to. But she refused to let his sexy smile and deep sultry voice lure her. He was her employee's nephew and she wanted…needed her paycheck. Still, there were times when she wondered…

"Have you told my uncle where I am?" His question interrupted her thoughts, which was probably for the best. She glanced around realizing he had parked in front of the Inn where she stayed.

"No. I don't believe he really cares *where* you are. He simply wants you back in Chicago."

"Did he give you a timeframe to find me and bring me back into the bosom of the family?" His voice was tinged with sarcasm.

"Three months, but I spent more than two of those trying to find a paper trail."

"Why?"

Cheyenne couldn't tell him her suspicions about Mr. Donovan's health. It was up to his uncle. But she couldn't lie, so she simply said, "That's the deadline your uncle gave me."

He tilted his head in contemplation. "So I have less than a month to consider."

Her shoulders drooped. "Why can't you just go now?"

He grinned, his eyes twinkling in the moonlight. "Because if I don't go, you won't go, will you?"

She narrowed her gaze.

"As I thought. So I have time to convince you that staying here on the island is better than living a life of duress in Chicago."

"You have a duty to maintain the reputation and legacy of the Donovan name."

Any signs of humor drained from his face, leaving his mouth pinched and furrows across his brow. Without a word, he got out of the jeep and came around to her side where he opened the door. But when she tried to get out, he blocked her path, hands on the seat back and dash.

He bent close and practically growled, "I thought we were going to leave further discussions for another day, but since you seem enamored with the Donovan name, get this simple fact straight. My name is not Donovan; my real name is Jake Smith."

She was sure her face showed her surprise, because as he stepped back, he said, "Look it up; February 12, 1998. Name changes aren't closed records, even for minors."

Leaving her standing barefoot on the boardwalk, clutching her ruined clothes, he jammed the vehicle into gear and drove off.

* * *

28

Cheyenne didn't bother grabbing a glass of wine to take up to her room. Besides the fact she didn't want anyone to see her in Joseph's – Jake's—clothes, she had some serious research to do. She quickly changed into her pajamas while her laptop booted up. She didn't think about calling Mr. Donovan. It was too late in the evening, for one thing, but it also had to do with privacy. She had worked for the man six years and never once had he mentioned that Joseph had been adopted, which no doubt meant he didn't want anyone to know.

Two hours later, Cheyenne stretched her arms over her head and yawned loudly. It hadn't been adoption but rather a custody issue she had found after going through countless databases and combing archival issues of the Chicago Tribune. Sebastian Everhart Donovan had filed for custody of ten year old Jake Smith on February 12, 1998 and had legally changed his name to Joseph Everhart Donovan. Cheyenne thought that rather egotistical since he wasn't the man's son but it was the custody matter that intrigued her. She knew Joseph's mother had been alive back then. (It would take a bit for her to think of him as Jake.) So why was Sebastian given custody?

She found her answer an hour later in a society column of the Tribune. Kathryn Donovan, renowned violinist had apparently broken down during a rehearsal for the Chicago Symphony and had quietly been ensconced at an elite and very private sanitarium. There was nothing else in the archives, though Cheyenne had done numerous searches.

Everything she read only led to more questions and while she should feel just a little guilty over snooping into her employer's life, she did not. After all, Jake had given her the initial information. If anything, she now felt some uneasiness over her brusque and unrepentant attitude toward Jake. She had the feeling there were reasons for his disappearance that she didn't understand.

She still intended to persuade him to return to Chicago. After all, she was employed by the senior Donovan and that was her job. But she thought there might be a better approach to the whole affair than threats and coercion.

* * *

Cheyenne stopped to dump sand from her shoes once again and decided to carry them. She had worn low heels today, but the shoes were still open-toed sling backs and considering there was sand everywhere, she might as well be barefoot. After all, it wasn't as though some Chicago Tribune reporter was following her around looking for photo ops. Besides, they would be more interested in a story about Jake, aka Joseph Donovan, than in her. Slipping her fingers through the shoes' thin straps, she smoothed down her skirt and continued to walk across the sand, her gaze never leaving her prey, now not more than ten yards away.

When Lindsay had dropped her off at the cottage, muttering all kinds of innuendos about who she was seeing and what they were doing, she had deliberately bypassed the door and headed for the dock. Besides, she had heard the sputtering sounds of a motor and she didn't want the man to get away from her. She had more questions than ever.

She stopped at the edge of the water, seriously contemplating dipping her feet into the cool blue. She glanced up to find his piercing brown gaze on her and decided it wouldn't do for her to be anything but totally professional. Even if she was barefoot at the moment.

"I see you have removed your shoes, Miss Tucker."

"I apologize for appearing so informal, but it's extremely difficult to walk otherwise. And I couldn't risk having you throw another pair in the water as fish food."

He gave a short laugh and she was glad his humor was back. She had not particularly cared for the dark side he had shown her last night.

"You keep asking me why I don't return to Chicago. Let me ask you a question."

She inclined her head.

30

"What do you feel?" He nodded to her bare feet and she could feel her embarrassment rising.

"Sand," she replied, her toes curling.

His gaze came back to hers; a sad and lonely look that poked at something in the region of her heart.

"And that is why."

He pulled the cord on the motor; once; twice, and when it roared to life he quickly flipped the mooring rope from the dock and slowly pulled away. His lips were moving but she couldn't hear what he said as he effectively dismissed her with another abrupt departure.

She stood at the edge of the water for several minutes, having absolutely no idea what he had been talking about. She pulled her cell out of her skirt pocket and called Lindsay to come pick her up. While she waited, she waded.

She was still barefoot and sitting on the porch step when Lindsay returned to take her back to town. Her crisply tailored shirt was wilted and tendrils of hair had escaped from her clip to drift across her face as the breeze blew.

"Girl, we have got to get you some clothes and sandals, maybe even a hat."

With a sigh, Cheyenne climbed onto the rickshaw seat. "I never intended to stay here very long; a few days at the most."

"And you're not leaving now because...?" She questioned as she steadily pedaled along the road. "Never mind," she continued when Cheyenne didn't immediately answer. "That hunk of a guy on the dock is changing your mind."

"His name is...Jake Smith," Cheyenne supplied.

"I know that. You can't be new on the island without getting checked out by most of the locals. In his case, my girlfriends and I have spent quite a few nights at the Gold Pelican watching him play."

"Play what; pool?"

Lindsay laughed. "He might do that, but I meant the piano. Cam has an old rinky-dink upright and I have to say

31

Jake's not bad. Not as good as Joseph Donovan, mind, but good enough to get some of the guys up and dancing."

A prick of envy had Cheyenne wiggling in her seat and before she could stop herself, she asked, "Does he dance, too?"

"No, he just drinks beer and plays for the crowd. I think he makes pretty good tips on the weekends." She turned to look over her shoulder. "It's tourist season so most of us do."

Cheyenne laughed, not so much at Lindsay's bold hint about tipping but more to think that any tips at all would make a difference to Jake who was worth millions.

When Lindsay stopped the rickshaw, Cheyenne realized they weren't at the Inn but rather down the street a few blocks where the shops and restaurants were located.

"Come on. This is the place to get you some clothes."

Cheyenne eyed the mannequins in the window display and hesitated. "I don't need a bikini and cover-up," she said.

"Well, you definitely need something more enticing than what you have been wearing if you want to lure Jake into being naughty and not running away from you every time you show up."

"I do not want; he doesn't…" Cheyenne sputtered.

Lindsay turned to her, hands on hips. "Didn't he leave you sitting at the bar the other day? And again just an hour ago?"

"How can you possibly know that?"

"Honey, this isn't Seattle or even Olympia. This is Lockabee, where everybody knows everybody *and* what they had for dinner last night.'"

"All right, but as for the rest of what you said…"

Lindsay had dragged her into the store by this time and there were several customers milling around. She lowered her voice. "Cheyenne, he brought you home last night and you were wearing his clothes." She raised a brow knowingly.

Cheyenne's stomach dropped to her toes. If Mr. Donovan ever caught a whiff of scandal concerning her; and especially with his nephew...

"You can't possibly think there was anything to that. You don't know the circumstances; nobody knows that. Why would anyone start such gossip?"

"I told you; it's Lockabee. Besides, most of the single women here, myself included, have tried to snag Jake's interest and haven't gotten to first base. So more power to you." She held up a sundress in a splash of bright colors. "Here. This is you."

Cheyenne had to admit the dress was pretty, if not something she could wear to work. And she was running out of clean clothes, even if she hadn't fallen in the water in her best suit.

In little over an hour, Lindsay had picked out, and Cheyenne had tried on what seemed like an entire wardrobe, including a comfortable pair of sandals and what she had called deck shoes.

"Wear the capris and blue print top," she said through the dressing room door. "Gotta take a call. Meet me out front."

Cheyenne donned the dark blue capris and top, strapping the sandals on. The top was cropped right to her waist and had narrow bands across the back. With the heat, she was more comfortable though casual, given her usual professional appearance. And although she was technically working, she wasn't in the formal offices of the Donovan Academy. Once she paid her bill and the clerk gave her two shopping bags, she looked for Lindsay outside. She was just hanging up her phone.

"I have to run," she said, reaching for the bags. "I'll drop these off at the Inn for you so you don't have to carry them to lunch."

"I wasn't planning on lunch," Cheyenne said.

Lindsay grinned. "You might want to change your mind." She swung onto her bike. "Later."

Cheyenne didn't have time to reply before a voice behind her called her name. She turned to see Jake step up onto the boardwalk.

"I'm through talking to you today," she caustically said, spinning around to head for the inn.

Jake had known she would probably be mad, thinking he had run out on her. He had hollered at her that he would be right back after taking the boat for a spin, but she was gone when he returned. That was why he had brought the boat around the inland waterway to the marina at Princetown. He had been hoping to catch her in town and apologize.

Now he grabbed her elbow as she walked away. "Wait."

She glared at him over the top of her sunglasses. "Excuse me?"

He released her, holding both hands in the air. "Give me a chance to explain," he paused before adding, "please?"

"Explain why you keep running away from me, or explain why you won't go back to Chicago where you belong?"

He should have known this wouldn't be easy. And he wasn't about to give her the answer to the first part of her question. The fact was Cheyenne Tucker scared him shitless. Not physically because she was a petite woman, but more because of his reaction to her. He had had a few affairs in his time, and even one two year relationship, but no one had gotten under his skin as quickly as the fair executive secretary. He had never seen her very often in Chicago. She had only been a fleeting, gossamer impression that rarely slipped into conscious thought.

Now, in the few days she had been on the island, she had invaded his dreams and all his waking hours. Although she kept trying to maintain a professional manner, he had begun to sense an underlying softness; especially after she had fallen off the dock and ended up in his clothes, her hair down and clean of makeup. She was tenacious, which he would have admired more if it wasn't so closely connected to capturing him like a fugitive. What he sensed the most and what drew him to her was her passion. If she could be so dedicated and determined at her job, what might she be like on a more personal, intimate level?

Jake knew he wanted to find out and yet it would invariably complicate things. All this sped through his head like *Flight of the Bumblebees* before he was pulled from his musings as she turned away from him and began walking again.

It was then he noticed her outfit. Gone was the professional Miss Tucker. Her slender spine was visible between blue flowered bands of a crop top, and slim calves and ankles showed in the capris she wore. Not that he hadn't seen her legs before, but the casual attire certainly made her more approachable. He would have to thank Lindsay, for he was sure this was her idea.

"You shouldn't be following me," she said without turning around. "I'm sure, even on Lockabee, there are laws against stalkers."

He lengthened his stride and pulled abreast of her. "Is this better?"

She glanced at him but didn't slow her pace. He took a second to admire her profile before offering her what she wanted.

"I'll tell you what you want to know if you'll have lunch with me."

"It's three in the afternoon. That's too late for lunch."

"Well, I haven't eaten so…" He put a hand to the small of her back and gently guided her into the restaurant they were passing, which was Brenda Kay's, his favorite place to eat. She didn't resist, which he took as a good sign.

Brenda Kay came over to wait on them as he slid into a booth opposite Cheyenne. She was a nice looking, middle-aged woman and had a friendly outgoing manner. Jake had liked her from the first time they met.

"Hello there, Jake. Ever get that boat of yours running? Harvey thinks he's ready to go fishing." Harvey, her husband, had health problems, which was one of the reasons they had retired and moved to the island. But

Brenda liked to keep busy and hadn't been content to garden, so had opened a restaurant.

"It puttered clear across the sound today," he said. "Old Hank wants to fish, too. Maybe I should start a fishing service. Might be able to make myself some money."

He heard Cheyenne give a choking sound and turned her way, narrowing his gaze. He didn't think she would give him away, but you never knew what went on in a woman's mind.

"This is Cheyenne, a…friend of mine. We'll have the fish and chips."

"Excuse me, but I think I can order for myself." She turned to Brenda Kay. "May I see a menu, please?"

Brenda raised a brow at Jake as though wondering where he had found her. He grinned and winked.

"You must be a tourist," Brenda Kay said as she pointed to a chalkboard above the bar, which contained only three items – hamburgers, barbeque ribs, and fish and chips.

Cheyenne sighed. "Fish and chips will be fine, and whatever light beer you have."

Jake was sure the surprise showed on his face. He was beginning to understand that the woman sitting across from him was extremely complex, and thought it might be fun to try and unravel and peel away the layers.

To begin with, he couldn't let her out drink him. "One for me, too, Brenda, but not the light."

She didn't say anything until their beers arrived. She took a sip, set it down and stared at him across the table. He had never realized how blue her eyes were; light in the center with dark rims. They were framed by dark lashes.

"Ok. You've got me here, now talk."

"We keep having the same conversation. You tell me why you're so dedicated to my uncle that you would fly half way across the country to find me."

"It's my job, and unlike some people, I take my responsibilities seriously."

"I have always taken my responsibilities seriously; until I decided enough was enough. Everyone's entitled to change jobs."

She sat with her mouth pinched as a waitress brought their food and another round of beers.

"May I have silverware, please?"

"You don't need it and we don't have it," the young girl said. "Nothing served requires it."

"Are you serious?" She gingerly fingered the brown paper wrap which crinkled as she opened it.

"It soaks up the grease," Jake told her. "Enjoy." He tipped his beer bottle toward her in salute.

He bit into a piece of the crisply fried fish and watched her eye the battered fish and golden French fries. She probably never ate fried food. Finally with a sigh she picked delicately at the fish.

"It is flaky and tender," she admitted.

"Brenda Kay's is the best around."

"Sans silverware," she retorted with a laugh, picking up a piece of fish and finally eating. She licked her fingers free of tartar sauce.

Jake watched her tongue snake out and everything in him tightened.

"You're not bad when you let your hair down," he said.

She reached up to pat her bun to make sure it was still in place.

"That's an expression," he said, "although maybe you should." He cocked his head to the side, studying her before reaching across the table and pulling the clip from her hair. Sunshine tumbled down around her shoulders.

She blushed prettily before ducking her head to concentrate on her meal. He continued watching her, somehow fascinated by her movements and the way her hair curled and swayed against her cheeks. His hands itched to touch it, wondering if it felt as soft as it looked. She finally raised her gaze back to his.

"Are you trying to distract me from the business at hand?" Her voice even sounded different; softer and somehow breathy.

There had often been times in Jake's life when a simple incident or object had triggered a melody in his head that wouldn't leave until he had spent hours; sometimes days without sleep, composing. This was suddenly one of those times. Notes and rhythms hummed in his brain, building into a burst of music.

"I have to go," he stated, downing the remains of his beer in a single swallow. He didn't fear the music would fade and he wouldn't be able to recapture it. Rather he couldn't wait to write it down; play it out and see if it sounded as wonderful out loud as it did in his head.

"Again?" She scowled at him.

The music had become almost frantic, and Jake didn't want to argue with her.

"I'm not running away. I promise not to leave the island," he said as he stood. "But there's something I have to do that won't wait."

He dropped several bills on the table, more than enough to pay for their meal. "I'll call you later; maybe come by."

"You are not leaving until we..." The rest of her statement was lost as Jake hurried out of the restaurant and down to the marina, chords and counterpoint chasing him all the way.

Chapter 4

Cheyenne sat dumbfounded as Jake walked out of the restaurant. She had no idea what caused his sudden departure yet again, but she was growing tired of chasing after him. She should simply call Mr. Donovan and give him Jake's location and be done with it.

Yet somewhere in the back of her mind, she sensed a disconnect between the two men. In the short time she had been pursuing Joseph Donovan, aka Jake Smith, he had become real, whereas before he had been a famous celebrity and somewhat unapproachable. Seeing him in a different environment made her more curious about the man behind the music. Since she had twenty-three more days before the deadline, she decided to bide her time and try to discover the truth.

"Your husband is hot," the young waitress commented as she stopped at the table to collect Jake's money.

"Hmm?" Her comment brought Cheyenne out of her revere. "Oh, he's not my...you think he's hot?"

The girl looked at her as though she were crazy, slid the money into her pocket and left. Cheyenne thought about the shaggy haired man who had just left. Even in cargo shorts and a tee shirt instead of a tuxedo, he exuded a masculinity that was hard to ignore. She thought about how her heart sped up whenever she was around him. Until now, she had thought it was because she was in awe of him and his talent, his family name and the whole mystic surrounding him. Now she wondered if it was something entirely different.

She brushed a lock of hair away from her cheek and automatically reached up to reposition the clip she wore but remembered Jake had removed it. Glancing across the table, she didn't see it. Why would Jake have taken her clip?

Instead of returning to the Inn, Cheyenne strolled along the narrow street of Princetown and looked in shop windows. It wasn't often she had the luxury of leisure time and felt somewhat guilty that she wasn't working. In Chicago, she had her weekends off, but usually spent them doing laundry and reading. The first year she had been there, she had explored the city and seen all the major sites. She wasn't much of a museum person, and had confined her wandering to the parks and what they called the Magnificent Mile. She had gone to Bloomingdale's once, and while she wore designer suits and shoes, she refused to pay the exorbitant prices just to say something came from the exclusive store.

She stopped in front of a store, looking at the toys in the window. Her nephew was five now, and with an ache, Cheyenne realized how much she missed the little tyke. Laramie had married right out of high school and Cheyenne had been at her wedding, but had left for Chicago shortly thereafter. She'd gone back to Sweetwater, Texas, every year since when she had a vacation, but those short visits now seemed very far away. She ached for the sticky little kisses and hugs Sammy used to give her. There was something about a child's innocence that pulled at her heart strings.

Impulsively, she entered the shop and looked around, wondering what a five year old liked in toys. She didn't know much about children. The ones who came to the Academy or who had private lessons with Mr. Donovan were more like miniature adults than children. Perhaps because of their musical talent and the practice and recital requirements, she doubted they had much time to play as normal children did. That made her think again about Jake. She knew he had been a prodigy, and now wondered if his

40

escape had not been an effort to have the *play time* he never had as a child.

When she saw small sailboats on a shelf, she thought that would be a fun gift. While Sweetwater didn't have any lakes and was certainly not near the gulf, she thought Sammy might like it to play in the bath. After ringing up her purchase, the saleslady told her where the post office was located. Considering Jake had disappeared, Cheyenne figured she had plenty of time to go back to the Inn and write a short letter to her sister to include with the toy. Tomorrow would be soon enough to mail the present.

Early the next morning, Cheyenne called Lindsay but it would be close to noon before she could be picked up. Apparently the weekenders were arriving on the ferry and it was an extremely busy time for the taxis. Even though Cheyenne paid her well, she couldn't blame the bicyclist for grabbing all the fares she could. After all, Cheyenne was rather a backup plan for when she wasn't busy elsewhere.

She slipped into her new pink capris and floral top, pulled her hair back into a ponytail and left the Inn in search of the post office. She felt carefree in the casual clothes. It wasn't that she never wore shorts or tees, but usually not out of the apartment. She had gotten so used to being professionally dressed for her job that even on weekends she usually wore dress slacks and blouses or sweaters. It had taken a long time to forget the hand-me-downs and patched clothes of her childhood, and she had promised herself with her first paycheck that her clothing allowance would be the majority of her salary.

Lindsay called just as Cheyenne came out of the post office and agreed to pick her up in half an hour at the marina across the street. Cheyenne hadn't paid much attention to the boat docks upon her arrival by ferry but now wandered along the sidewalk surveying the yachts and motorboats moored in various slips. One yacht even had what could only be a heliport on the very top. Cheyenne shook her head, unable to fathom the kind of money that must be had by various residents of the island.

"Hey, girl. Looking sharp." Lindsay braked to a halt on the street next to the bench where Cheyenne had settled. "Where are we off to today?"

Cheyenne liked the cyclist, partly because of her casual attitude. She was friendly and put no store in appearances, as depicted by her ragged cutoffs, tank top and red hair pulled through the back of a ball cap. Today her rickshaw was a two row, four-seater and Cheyenne wondered how she managed to tote four people and luggage around.

"Do you have time for a trip to Crystal Bay?"

Lindsay grinned. "Off on a little rendezvous?"

Cheyenne knew Lindsay thought Jake and she had a fling going, and rather than explain the real reason she was here; and Jake's real identity, she decided to play along.

"Not yet, but there's always hope." The words caused a curious roll of her stomach and a skip of her heart. Surely she didn't want anything romantic to happen with Jake, did she?

She wasn't about to find out that day. When they got to the cottage, Cheyenne had Lindsay wait while she checked the house. The curtains were all closed so she couldn't see in and the doors were locked. She walked around to the back and saw that the boat was at the dock. His jeep was nowhere to be seen, but that could mean he was anywhere on the island and Cheyenne wasn't about to spend an entire day in the heat looking for him.

"Where is that place you said he goes to play the piano?" she asked Lindsay as she climbed back onto the seat.

"The Gold Pelican?" She started down the road.

"Take me there, would you?"

"Got it."

She wouldn't spend the entire day looking for him, but it wouldn't hurt to check one or two of the places he frequented.

She let Lindsay go when they reached town, as the entire front street was only three blocks in length. She stepped into the Gold Pelican and stood a minute, letting her eyes adjust to the dim interior. No piano music greeted her, and although the place was almost full of people, not one of them was Jake. She approached the bartender.

"Has Jake been around?"

"Want a beer?" He answered her question with one of his own.

"No, I don't want a beer. What is it with you people?"

He shrugged. "Gotta make a living."

She waited to see if he would answer her question. When someone called from the other end of the bar, he turned and left. *How rude*, she thought, but then she had the feeling he was a friend of Jake's, so shouldn't have been surprised.

There was nothing left to do but return to the Inn. She visited with the hostess, Mrs. Godfrey, to insure she could keep her room another week. Surely by that time she could convince Jake to return to Chicago, if only to see what his uncle wanted.

When she got to her room, her computer light was blinking, indicating she had email. She hesitated before opening it, as she didn't want to address any questions from Mr. Donovan and she certainly couldn't lie. She was actually surprised that he hadn't called her by this time.

The message was short and curt – "*I assume I will hear from you soon. In the meantime, take care of business.*" There were several attachments which included letters that needed answers, invoices that needed paid, and inquiries to be addressed. Cheyenne was slightly affronted by his attitude, even as she reminded herself that she was his executive assistant and it was her job to *take care of business*.

Wasn't that what she was doing? She muttered as she kicked off her sandals and settled down to work. She didn't realize how long she sat there until she glanced up and noticed the room was relatively dark. She switched on the lights and glanced at the clock. There was still no word from Jake, even though she had called several times. His phone went straight to voice mail, but she refused to leave a message. She didn't want him to think she was groveling.

Deciding she was hungry, she grabbed her purse and went downstairs. The small parlor was full of chattering people, enjoying a glass of wine. She wasn't a typically social person, and knew the residents were tourists, so they held little interest for her. They wouldn't know where to find the illusive musician.

As she walked past the Gold Pelican, she heard music so popped in hoping Jake was at the piano. Unfortunately it was a woman playing some vaguely familiar tune that stuck in Cheyenne's head as she walked further down the street. Princetown looked different in the twilight. There were no neon street lights but instead the buildings were outlined in strings of white lights and small old fashioned style lanterns were at the corners. The street was crowded with foot traffic as well as cyclists. Everyone was chatting in groups ranging from a couple to a half dozen or more. It made her feel rather lonely. She didn't often go out by herself for that very reason and she almost turned back without eating but her stomach growled at the same time she caught a whiff of barbeque.

She stopped at a bistro to read the menu posted outside. They offered several choices of steak, and the smell was delicious. There was no wait and she soon sat at a small table by a back window overlooking the marina, sipping a glass of white wine.

"Your dinner, Miss." The voice came from behind her as a lean brown hand holding a steak plate came into view. Her wine glass clattered to the table, and she grabbed it before it tipped. She glanced briefly at the steak and twice baked potato before looking up into laughing brown eyes.

"May I join you?" He held another plate containing a much larger steak than her filet.

"I suppose it won't be like having real company for dinner as you'll probably run off in the middle of it." She took a sip of wine to settle the butterflies in her stomach. He assumed that was her consent, and slid into the chair across from her.

"Surely you don't work here," she said.

He raised a brow as he cut into his steak. "What would be wrong with that?"

"You certainly don't need the money."

He shrugged. "There are plenty of reasons to work besides money. I enjoy meeting people. But no, I don't work here. I happened to be passing by when I saw you walk in so I asked the chef if I could bring out your meal."

"You know the chef?"

"It's a small island."

"Yet large enough for you to hide," she couldn't help replying.

He smiled. "You have a sharp tongue, Miss Tucker."

She ignored him in favor of her steak. At the first bite, she was in heaven. Juicy and so tender it melted in her mouth, she didn't stop until she had consumed more than half. When she finally put down her knife and fork to drink, she looked across the table to find Jake staring at her, a funny look on his face. Her cheeks burned with embarrassment.

"I was hungry," she said defensively.

He laughed gently. "Don't apologize. I enjoy eating as much as the next person and it's good to see a lady do the same. There's nothing I hate worse than someone ordering a meal then taking only a bite or two and claiming they're full."

She didn't ask but assumed he was referring to previous dates he'd had. Not that this was a date.

"In fact, I'm the one who should be apologizing," he continued. "Which I seem to be doing a lot since you came."

"It would be easy enough to rid yourself of that habit if you would quit leaving every time I come across you."

He looked to the side as though in thought before returning his gaze to her. "There's supposed to be what they call a blue blood super moon along with the lunar eclipse tonight. Will you come out to the cottage with me to see it? There should be an unobstructed view across the water."

She knew he was changing the subject and wondered why. Her brain instinctively told her going to a cabin, at night, with a handsome man was probably not the best idea. When she hesitated, he gave her his winning grin and added, "As long as you're stuck with me and vice-versa for twenty-some more days…"

Since he seemed determined not to give in until the very last minute, perhaps spending time with him would give her some insight as to why it was so important for him to separate himself from his uncle. At least that was what she told herself as they got up to leave the restaurant.

It was fully dark by the time they walked outside. "This way," Jake said, putting a hand to her back to steer her down the street. "Once tourist season starts, the streets become pedestrian and bike traffic only. I had to park over a few blocks." He glanced down as she walked beside him. "At least you have practical shoes on tonight."

He wasn't going to let her forget the disaster on the dock, and she wasn't going to let him off the hook for throwing her shoes in the bay. "You will find the cost of my shoes deducted from your next paycheck. That is, if you decide to return and actually earn one."

He laughed; a loud, happy laugh that shook him and vibrated down his arm and onto her back, sending a shiver up her spine. She had to admit his laughter wasn't something she was used to, and the sound coursed through her like potent whiskey. She had never thought of him as an eligible man in Chicago. Now, she was finding him not only eligible, at least according to Lindsay, but very approachable. The thought scared her and she decided to return to the Inn and forego his invitation. Before she could form a thought, they came to his Jeep and he held the door open for her. After a moment's hesitation, she got in, unable to resist temptation.

It took only a few minutes to get to his cottage. He opened the door for her and flipped on the lights as she entered.

"You don't lock your doors?"

"Not always. This isn't Chicago. Except for my clothes and a few other items, there's nothing I have to lose."

He walked to the refrigerator. "Want a beer?"

She hesitated but decided she could handle one. "Sure." As he opened a couple of bottles, she noticed a keyboard and papers scattered across the table.

"You're composing." She picked up a page. Being able to read music wasn't part of her job description, so she had no idea of the melody. "You haven't totally left your profession?"

He lifted a shoulder in a shrug as he handed her a beer. "I compose and play because I do love it. I left performing because I refused to let it, or my uncle, control my life any longer."

"Which is why I'm here." She took a swallow of beer before continuing. "Joseph," she started but at his look, she recanted. "Jake, we really do need to talk about things. Your uncle wants you back in Chicago, and—"

"Not now," he interrupted. "The moon is coming up and we'll miss the eclipse." He led her through the small living room to a back door, and out onto a deck that faced the bay. A telescope sat on the back edge. There was a small table and two chairs along with a chimenea.

"Have a seat." He set his beer bottle on the table and went over to light the wood that had been stacked inside the terra cotta fire place.

Instead of sitting, she walked over to the telescope and peered through the eye piece.

"I didn't know you had an interest in astronomy."

"All my uncle ever let me do was practice and perform. He saw little use for more than basic education. From the beginning, he would say 'the world will focus on your compositions, not whether you have ever read Tom Sawyer.' But I would sneak down to the library and hide books under my bed, staying up all hours devouring anything I could get my hands on."

"When did you start playing?"

"When I was six, although my uncle didn't know about it at first."

"That was when you were a child. You're, what, thirty years old now? Until you left two months ago, you had no free will?"

"Look, the eclipse has started." He walked up to where she stood by the telescope. "Have a look."

"It's not really doing much," she said, squinting up into the night. He stepped aside and she peered through the lens. "Everything's fuzzy."

He stepped close behind her, reaching around to a knob on the side of the instrument. She could smell his aftershave, a woodsy scent that tingled her nose and made her think very inappropriate thoughts. He took a breath, his chest barely touching her back, but the contact was sizzling.

"Is that better?" he whispered close to her ear. He didn't move and she couldn't breathe.

"Cheyenne?" A hand came to rest on her shoulder as she swayed. "Are you okay?"

"Hmm? Oh." Her body absorbed everything about him and she had the insane thought that he might kiss her. She quickly stepped away. When he gave her a curious look, she said the first thing that came to mind. "It's rather like watching grass grow, isn't it?"

He laughed. "The entire process of a total eclipse such as this takes awhile from the time the earth's shadow starts across the moon until it's completely covered, then slips to the other side. The period of totality is only about seven and a half minutes. So, yes, it is rather slow, but still one of the world's wonders. It makes me think of an adagio; a slow piece of music."

"Which brings us right back to where we were." She turned to look him directly in the eyes. "Jake, your uncle sent me to find you and bring you home. Please tell me why you won't go."

He rubbed a hand over his face, his brown eyes too dark to read in the diminishing moonlight. With a sigh, he took her hand and led her back to the small table.

"Have a seat and let me tell you a story."

Chapter 5

He took the seat across from her after adding more wood to the fire.

"How much do you know about our family?"

"Very little, I suppose. I've worked several years for your uncle, but strictly as his executive assistant. He's never spoken about the family."

"My uncle is a composer. He's done several musical scores for film and a ton of commercials, but the big prizes – a Grammy or Tony – have always eluded him. That made him even more determined when he found out I could play." He sipped his beer and she watched him. His brow wrinkled and she wondered if he had decided not to tell her more.

"Let me back up. Sebastian raised his sister, my mother, after their parents died when they were in their teens. He trained her on the violin and she was playing for the Chicago Philharmonic Orchestra by the time she was eighteen. She was quite good but never liked the pressure of public performances. She ran off when she was twenty, ended up pregnant with me and only returned to her brother because his private investigator found her."

Cheyenne said nothing when he glanced her way. Having grown up with a mother and no father, she certainly wasn't one to judge.

"My uncle insisted she continue to play, though she didn't perform publicly except on rare occasions. I would sneak into the music room while she was practicing. I loved to listen to her, but more, I loved to watch her. It was like she was entranced, standing there in that large room, eyes closed, body swaying with the music. She was how I imagined an angel would look. She was my angel."

Again, he stopped, turning to contemplate the fire. Cheyenne could almost feel his pain, as though speaking the words pulled something from deep inside him. When he turned back, she could swear his eyes glittered with tears.

"I hid under the grand piano once when Uncle came in. I'm sure he saw me, but he didn't say anything, perhaps because I seemed to be a source of pleasure for my mother. She would look at me sometimes with a smile and the tempo of her music would pick up, as though she knew I wanted happy music.

"When I was six, she was playing a particularly difficult piece and kept stopping and restarting. I instinctively knew where the music was going, so I climbed onto the piano bench and started playing the next refrain. She turned to stare at me and I continued to play. I thought she would be happy that I knew the music, but a horrified expression crossed her face and she set her violin aside and rushed over to where I sat. She grabbed my hands and slammed the cover shut on the keys. I didn't think I had done anything wrong, but when I looked up at her, she was crying. She sank down on the bench beside me and cuddled me close, her whole body shaking.

"'You mustn't tell Sebastian you can play'," she whispered to me. "'Promise me you will never, never tell.'"

"You were a prodigy," Cheyenne said. "You have a natural gift. Why did your mother not want you to pursue it?"

"She never said, but I would guess because she knew how hard Sebastian would push me and how he would exploit my talent."

"I always wished I could play the piano," she said, "but I never had an opportunity." She didn't mean for her comment to sound sarcastic, but he took it that way.

"It's not that I don't like music; it is my passion. However, I could no longer stand the confining atmosphere of practicing and performing; never having a moment to myself; always being on display."

"I can understand that, I guess," she agreed, but she wanted more of the story. "So how did your uncle find out if you weren't supposed to tell?"

"From the moment I touched the keys, a whole world opened for me. My mother seemed to understand, but she would only let me play when Sebastian wasn't home. I have perfect pitch and an eidetic memory, so all she had to do was play a short piece once and I knew it by heart."

Jake paused for a moment, glancing up at the moon. "Look; it's almost a complete eclipse."

Cheyenne looked up, surprised at not having noticed the darkness. Only a tiny sliver of moon was visible in the night sky. As they watched, that, too, disappeared for a brief time before a little light appeared on the opposite side.

"Thank you for asking me out here tonight," she said softly. "I've never taken time to ..." she paused, not wanting to talk about herself. She was much more interested in Jake's story.

"To watch grass grow," Jake finished her sentence with a laugh.

She joined in. "Well, that too." She hesitated before continuing. "Will you tell me the rest?"

"After another beer," he said, getting up to go inside.

She heard the door shut when he returned, but still jumped when his arm brushed her shoulder as he handed her another cold one. Something had shifted between them. They no longer seemed pursuer and pursued, but simply a man and woman. She gulped down several swallows of beer, trying to drown the butterflies.

"So there I was, a six year old addict, but addicted to music that came out of nowhere. It was always inside my head, spinning and swirling until I thought I would go mad if I didn't give voice to the notes. The thing was, I didn't want to play Beethoven or Chopin. I heard things for which there was no score. One day I was in the music room playing something I had composed and my uncle caught me. Given my mother's talent, he didn't seem surprised that I could play but when he asked the name of the piece, I made the mistake of saying that I hadn't titled it yet."

51

He laughed, but it was a hurtful sound. "That did surprise him. From that moment, he wouldn't allow my mother to enroll me in public school. I spent all my time at the piano under his tutelage, and only through my mother's stand against him did I even learn to read and write."

Cheyenne thought of her own mother, who hadn't seemed to care for either of her children and in fact, had run off when Cheyenne was just sixteen. "Knowing your uncle the little that I do, your mother must have been a very strong woman."

He shook his head. "She wasn't, really. My uncle badgered her, ranting because she wouldn't perform with my accompaniment. He wanted to tout us like some Barnum and Bailey act. Then, when I was ten, she tried to take her own life."

Cheyenne gasped. "The papers never said that." The words slipped out.

He gave her a sad smile. "I see you've done your research. Of course, Uncle covered it up, stating that she had a physical breakdown and had gone to an exclusive resort to rest. While she was gone, he filed for custody and officially adopted me, changing my name." The last was said in anger.

"I never met your mother, but it was my understanding that she lived in the house. So I assume you continued to see her."

"Oh, yes. She was only in the sanitarium for a year, but it was long enough for my uncle to brainwash me, telling me it had been my fault, and if I didn't continue to play and compose, she would get sick again."

"Oh, Jake. I am so sorry." She was beginning to have a very different view of the Donovans, particularly Sebastian.

He shrugged off her sympathy. "I did what I had to do, which was practice an average of ten hours a day."

"Ten hours?"

"Do you know what happened when I refused?"

"Your teacher rapped your fingers with a ruler?" It was a flippant reply but she couldn't think of anything except a little boy trying to please someone who she was beginning to think couldn't be pleased.

He held his hands up, wiggling his fingers. "These hands? God forbid anyone touch these money making digits. These hands never played sports, welded a knife to whittle or punched a bully in the mouth. Nothing that could possibly damage even a single, tiny nail. No, my uncle would refuse to let me see my mother."

Cheyenne didn't know what to say. Her own parent had been thoughtless and negligent but she hadn't been abusive in the way Sebastian Donovan had.

"So now, my dear Miss Tucker, you know why I left. I feel my uncle is responsible for my mother's demise. The best way to get back at him was to quit playing, which I would never do while my mother was alive. Even now, the only way I could quit was to run away."

Cheyenne got up and walked to the edge of the porch, looking out to where the water of the bay lapped gently at the sand. Things had become awkward now. She was employed by Sebastian Donovan, yet she found it hard to think about convincing Jake to return to Chicago after hearing his story. On the other hand, she thought about Mr. Donovan's failing health, though he had never said he was ill. Should she tell Jake, although she had been warned not to do so? She now understood his animosity, but if she didn't convince him to return and the older Donovan died, would he regret not making amends?

A warm hand touched her shoulder, turning her around. He stood very close, and when she didn't step back, his arms circled her. She looked up, her gaze tracing the fine curve of his lips; lips that were descending toward her own.

"I didn't tell you my story to make you sad," he said. A kiss, as light as the breeze, touched the corner of her mouth. "I simply wanted you to know." Another kiss to the other side.

"Everything is complicated now." She watched his lips curve into a smile.

"It doesn't have to be. Let's pretend," he pulled her gently forward, "we're just an ordinary guy and gal enjoying a full moon and night sky."

She made a choked sound. "You are hardly an ordinary guy."

He kissed her forehead and she ached to tug his mouth back to hers. "That's the wonderful thing about pretend." He kissed her nose. "You can be anything you want."

She had never been seduced by a simple kiss before, but her legs were wobbling. She curled her arms up along his back for support as his mouth covered hers. His kiss was like his music, vibrant and seductive. His firm lips slanted across hers, drawing her deeper into the night where anything was possible. She opened as his tongue slid across her lips and she was lost.

Somewhere in the night an owl hooted and the wood in the fire popped; both sounding louder than usual. Cheyenne felt all of her senses come alive as the kiss went from gentle to demanding, his tongue flicking in to tangle with her own. His hands slid under her top to caress her bare back. She knew she should stop, but the caress felt so good. It had been so long since she had been in any kind of relationship. Was it wrong to want that?

Then she remembered who she was kissing. She was an employee of Donovan Academy of Music, and he was the most famous Donovan of all. She slid her hands around to his chest and pushed. This was not why she was here, she reminded herself, even as her body bemoaned the loss of contact when he released her.

"I think I should go back to town." She choked the words out, not actually wanting that, but knowing it was for the best.

"I think you should stay." He tucked his hands in his front pockets and simply looked at her.

"You don't know what you're asking."

He grinned. "Oh, but I do. And you, fair Miss Tucker, don't know what you're missing."

* * *

In the end, Jake took Cheyenne back to town and dropped her safely off at the Inn. She probably thought he was mad because he didn't talk the few minutes it took to drive to town, but his head was spinning with music and he couldn't have carried on a conversation if he had tried. This was the second time that had happened when he was with her, and all he could think was to get back to the cottage, write down the notes and play them to see if the melody sounded as beautiful as she looked.

He had never had trouble composing, but in recent years original scores had been a struggle. His concert performances were entirely made up of works he had created before. In the past year when his mother had been so ill, he had quit composing entirely. Although he had told Cheyenne he had quit playing to spite his uncle, that hadn't been entirely true. He had no longer found the joy in music that his mother had instilled in him. His vision of her playing had faded to a point where he ached for that little boy who would sit and listen to her for hours. Then she died, and the music in his head had quit.

Until now. He hurried into the cottage and sat in front of the small keyboard on the table. It didn't quite have the sound of his grand piano, but it would do for now. He closed his eyes as he caressed the keys, recalling the tentativeness of Cheyenne's kiss. He didn't think she was a complete innocent, but she certainly wasn't a seductress. Yet there was a sweetness in her that called to him. That charming appeal had his fingers racing across the keyboard first in a capriccio and then rolling into a smooth legato, the last note lingering in the night.

Not quite there, he thought, as he jotted down a string of musical notes on paper. Beside the first refrain, he noted the instruments. This would not be a simple piano solo. He picked up the pages he had completed the other night, scanning them to see if the rhythm fit with what he had just done. The melody was there, full and rich, and would work well for a full orchestra.

He worked until his eyes crossed, stopping only to make a quick sandwich and slug some coffee down. When he finally crawled into bed over twenty-four hours later, the sun was creeping above the horizon. He dreamed of Cheyenne, and how to get passed the prickliness to the real woman within.

His thoughts were still on her when he arose after sleeping the day away. There was something connecting them and although he couldn't define it, he accepted it was there. The problem was to get Cheyenne to see what to him was plain as day. He knew she had issues with who he was, so he had to convince her that he was just an ordinary mortal, not some super mega-man as he was portrayed in the media.

His phone rang before he had time to formulate a plan.

"I know it's short notice but Crazy Daisy left for Seattle an hour ago and I could use a player as there'll be *for'ners* in for the weekend and all that," Cam, bartender at the Gold Pelican, said in one long sentence.

Most Lockabee islanders had their own particular lingo, and it had taken him weeks before he understood half of what they said. The woman Cam Bristol referred to was actually Delilah Murray, a former Broadway actress who loved singing bawdy songs and was a favorite at the bar. *For'ners,* a shortened form of foreigners, was the most often used word for tourists, and *player* was, of course, a piano player.

"Tonight?"

"No, two weeks from Sunday is short notice," he sarcastically replied. "Do I have to start calling you a *for'ner* again?"

Jake laughed. "All right. Give me time to grab a shower and I'll be in, but it'll cost you a steak as I haven't eaten."

"I'll see you shortly." The phone clicked.

He found the sticky note on his windshield when he climbed into the Jeep thirty minutes later. Of course she would carry sticky notes. *Don't ignore me, Jake. I'm not going away!!!* Three exclamation points; she had to be really mad. He must have been totally in the zone if she had knocked on the door and he hadn't heard her because there was no way he could ignore Miss Cheyenne Tucker. He pulled out his phone and sent her a text. This was the perfect opportunity for her to see him as an ordinary guy.

Chapter 6

Cheyenne paced around the small room as she had been doing most of the evening. The more she thought about Jake's behavior, the madder she got. How dare he kiss her senseless, then not talk to her the entire way to town, then completely ignore her for the following two days.

All right, she might not have been completely senseless because she did manage not to let things go too far. But his comment about her not knowing what she was missing? That had led to her tossing and turning all that night, her body hot with unfulfilled sexual desire. When he didn't call the next day, she thought it just as well when she noticed the dark circles under her eyes. She had spent that day doing correspondence and email. The second day, she had gone out to the cottage but when he didn't answer her knocks, she left him a note. Time was running out. She had less than twenty days to convince him to return to Chicago.

And that brought up a whole new set of problems. After hearing his story, she couldn't really blame him for not wanting to see his uncle. On the other hand, how could he justify throwing away his career and the talent he had.

Her phone pinged and like an eager teenager, she dove across the bed to retrieve it.

Meet me at the Gold Pelican.

That was it? No apology for ignoring her; no *please*? Well, if he wanted to go back to formal and impersonal, so could she. She dressed in her best suit and heels, applied a striking shade of red lipstick and headed out into the night.

The small village was overrun with people as she started down the street. The entire narrow lane seemed like one large party even though it was already after ten in the evening. Apparently everyone wanted to make the most of their time on the island.

It wasn't hard to find the Gold Pelican, and not because she had been there before. The large wooden bird hanging at an angle was flashing with bright lights and singing could be heard half a block away as the double doors were flung wide. Inside, it was crowded but not packed, so she made her way to the bar. Against her most fervent hope, the same bartender was on duty as had been on her previous visits; however he was civil as he asked if she wanted a beer.

"Do you have white wine?" she asked. At his nod, she said she would take that.

Whatever song the crowd had been singing had ended, but almost immediately another tune started. The music was loud and slightly off-key but the many patrons sitting around scar topped tables and at the long waist high bar didn't seem to mind as many of them sang along. She couldn't see the piano player from her spot at the bar, nor could she see Jake when she scanned the crowd.

The bartender came back with her wine and she took a sip, mildly surprised by the quality. She handed the man a twenty and when he brought her change, she left it on the bar, hoping it would buy her some information.

"I'm looking for Jake," she said.

The man narrowed his gaze. "That so?"

She couldn't blame him for being cautious giving out information as she hadn't been exactly forthcoming in their first encounter. She quickly added, "He asked me to meet him here."

Instead of answering, he jerked his head toward the back of the bar.

"He went out the back way, again?"

He laughed, picked up her change, and said, "Follow me," as he headed down the bar.

Cheyenne quickly grabbed her wine to follow. One man whistled at her and another tried to grab her arm as she skirted the crowd standing or sitting by the bar. At the other end, he tapped a man on the shoulder, said something she couldn't hear over the music, and the man got off his stool and waved her to it. Grateful, she smiled her thanks and sat, once again facing the bartender.

"Well?" she asked, thinking he would give her an explanation as to why she had moved or where Jake was.

"I got to do everything for you *for'ners*?" he questioned.

Cheyenne's eyes widened. Surely he hadn't just called her an inappropriate word?

"Turn your little ass around, missy."

Too stunned to reply, she actually did as he said. And there was Jake, not more than ten feet away from her, banging away on an old upright piano in the back corner. Fascinated, she watched as he played one shouted request after the other. He seemed to know every song, whether it was some moody fifties tune or a modern hip-hop melody.

He continually sipped from a mug of beer, although as she observed him, the level of the beverage didn't seem to diminish. This was Jake Smith, she realized, not Joseph Donovan. This was the ordinary man he professed he wanted to be. It made no difference that he probably only got paid in beer and tips; he was all smiles, having a grand time. Her gaze traveled to his hands, ardently caressing the piano keys and suddenly, all she could think about was what those fingers would feel like on her skin. Would he be as energetic in love making as he was playing ballsy ballads for the patrons?

She knew her face heated, and as though drawn to her because of her thoughts, he lifted his head and found her among the crowd. His smile widened and he winked, which only made her blush harder. He finished the song with a flourish and stood. The crowd was already shouting out song titles but he shook his head, holding up one hand. Apparently even able to mesmerize this rowdy crowd, the noise quickly dissipated.

60

"I'm taking a break, folks," he said. "Have a beer and some of the Gold Pelican's famous fried oysters and clams, and I'll be back shortly."

He headed her way, although his progress was slow as people claimed his attention. She watched him closely and realized yet another facet of Jake, not Joseph. This man liked people, not the attention of being famous. No one knew him here with his long hair and casual clothes. He wasn't trying to impress the audience so they would buy his albums and attend more concerts. In fact, he was a walking advertisement for the Gold Pelican, not the Donovan Academy of Music.

He stopped beside her stool. "You came," he said, and she heard surprise in his voice.

She turned slightly toward him. "I always do what I'm told," she replied, referring to his abrupt text. Her comment caused a laugh.

"I seriously doubt that." And then she was the one surprised as he leaned over and kissed her, right on the mouth, in front of everyone. There were a few hoots from the crowd and she realized they were the center of attention. She could feel the blush creep up her neck but Jake didn't appear at all embarrassed as he laughed again and ordered a red beer from the bartender, along with another wine for her.

"This is why I haven't heard from you in days?" she asked, more for want of a better topic of conversation.

He shook his head. "Cam called tonight with an emergency so I came to fill in. I don't play here often." He sipped his beer and said nothing more.

"We should probably talk about what happened the other night." The comment simply popped out, but really, his kiss at the cottage had come out of nowhere and her response had totally astonished her. And now he had kissed her again, as though they were...dating. While she had dreamed of nothing but him and taking the kiss further, he seemed rather casual about it all.

Yet at her comment, his gaze darkened and a slow smile lifted the corners of his mouth. He leaned closer and whispered in her ear, "You really don't want to have that conversation here, do you?" His breath was warm and his lips touched her ear lobe, causing heat to sizzle down her spine.

"I'm not paying you to neck with the customers," the bartender said sarcastically.

Jake laughed again, apparently in too good a mood to let anything bother him. "You aren't paying me at all, Bristol." He downed the rest of his beer, then added, "I'm doing you a favor, remember?"

"Then do it."

Jake turned to her. "Will you stay? I have to play until one or after."

"Why do you *have to*, if it's a favor? And is he always so cynical?"

Instead of answering her, he leaned in for yet another kiss. "Stay?"

She pinched her lips, not in displeasure but to try and hold in the taste of him. When she gave him a nod, he traced her cheek with a finger and then he was gone; back to his merry band of singers. She watched him start to play and immediately several couples got up to dance while others sang loudly. He was like the Pied Piper, she thought as she lifted her fingers to trace the path his lips had taken on hers.

She had never been a groupie. While she had listened to an old radio at home, she could never afford buying albums or going to concerts and she really didn't have a favorite artist. In fact, her tastes ran about as far from the latest billboard charts as could be – to Raga and Bluegrass. Of course, she had listened to Donovan's music, as it was usually softly playing in the background at the office.

Now, she sat there thoroughly enjoying his performance, though of course it wasn't his own music. It was him she enjoyed watching for he was truly in his element. She again wondered why his uncle wanted him back in Chicago. Was it only for the Camelot competition that Jake had said Sebastian wanted him to enter? But from what she was witnessing, Jake had found another avenue of music to pursue. Was that bad, to allow his gift to take him down a different path? But, where did that leave her? She couldn't force him to return and she couldn't tell him of her suspicions regarding his uncle's health. She would have to appeal to his sense of honor.

The crowd had become rowdier, which wasn't unusual for a weekend, so Jake played a few slower songs, hoping to bring things to a peaceful conclusion as it approached closing time. He had kept an eye on Cheyenne, hoping she would stay so he could drive her home, but just as he started yet another melody of classics, a tall, bearded man slid an arm around her from the back. He said something that widened her eyes, then he smacked his lips and leaned toward her.

Jake stood, still playing as he watched Cheyenne immediately straighten and slam an elbow into his midsection. Good girl, he thought, but her actions only made the man laugh and tighten his hold. Cheyenne pushed hard against his chest to no avail and Jake lost it.

With a roar he slammed both hands against the keyboard, surprising those close to him but he didn't stop to worry about it. A dozen strides and Jake grabbed the man by the hair and twisted, eliciting a yowl. The ruffian released Cheyenne but turned on Jake, yanking his hand free and squeezing it. Pain shot up his arm, but he reared back with the other fist and slammed it into the man's face.

Chaos was immediate and rampant. The crowd that had once been happily singing started punching any nearby body. Chairs scrapped and glass crashed to the floor. Jake shoved Cheyenne against the bar, standing between her and the man who had accosted her. Another man, a tourist from the looks of his loud floral shirt, came up to assist, but got roughly pushed aside. The fighting was going on across the entire tavern now; cameras flashed and people yelled but Jake concentrated on one person. He could hear the sirens, and knew the sheriff would be there quickly but he wasn't done with anyone who would lay a hand on Cheyenne. He hit him again, this time right in the mouth, and his hand came back bloody. He shook it and swore.

"You bastard!" Cheyenne shouted at the man. "Do you have any idea who he is?"

Out of the corner of his eye, Jake saw her reach for a beer bottle on the bar. Before he could stop her, she swung it, smashing the man on the side of the head. When that didn't stop him, she hit him again. Jake made the mistake of turning to subdue her.

A flying chair hit him in the back of the head and he started to slump to the floor. His last conscious thought, as yet another camera flashed in his face, was that he was going to miss how this all ended.

* * *

Cheyenne was politely escorted into a cell with several other women. The men were in a holding cell down a narrow corridor. She had tried to explain things to the Sheriff but considering she still had a beer bottle in her hand when he and a deputy managed to calm the chaos at the bar, she had been one of the first to be taken away. Her last glimpse of Jake had tears streaming down her face. He was propped up against the bar with his friend, Cam, squatted by him, a towel pressed against his cheek. He had another towel wrapped around his right hand.

She might have to spend the night in jail; indeed, she could very well lose her job over what had happened, but she would do it all again. All she could think about was Jake's hand. She had seen blood on it after he had punched that bully, but she didn't know if it was his or the other man's. Regardless, his hands; his livelihood had been damaged.

The fact that it was all her fault caused her stomach to clutch to the point she was sure she would throw up. She had never been in a fight much less caused one. She knew that Jake had been trying to come to her rescue, and while normally she carried mace in her purse, she had not tonight.

Besides, who would have thought that in a quiet little seaside town, she would need to protect herself.

One by one, the other women were released as their husbands or friends came to retrieve them, some of them after having been released themselves. Finally, she sat alone, trying to smooth the wrinkles out of her skirt; noticing the beer stain that ran along the left side, and generally feeling sorry for herself. She didn't have anyone to call except Jake and she didn't know if he would bail her out. He might not even be able to if he had been badly hurt.

Oh, god, she thought, he might even be in the hospital.

Tears welled up and spilled down her cheeks. She swiped at the moisture and the hair hanging in her face. She had lost her clip in the fray, and the sheriff had confiscated her purse so she didn't even have a comb. When she heard voices down the hall, she smoothed her hair the best she could and straightened her suit jacket. It was about time the sheriff saw to letting her make a phone call.

She stood, determined to make her displeasure known, but it wasn't the sheriff who came to a stop in front of the cell.

"Well, well, Miss Tucker. Is this any way for the executive assistant to Sebastian Donovan to spend her time?" Jake leaned a shoulder against the bars, one hand tucked in his front pocket. The other hand, swathed in white bandages, hung at his side. There was a bruise on his cheek and a small split on his lip. He looked wonderful to her eyes and yet she snapped at him for the ridiculous way he said her name.

"Quit calling me Miss Tucker. It makes me sound like an old school teacher."

"Well you dress like it in those suits." He waved his hand at her.

"I dress for my job. Your uncle insists on a certain look."

"My uncle insists on a lot of things, not always in the best interest of those concerned.

If it were me, I would insist on shorts and tee shirts, although the heels are nice. They make your legs look great."

To cover her embarrassment, she replied caustically, "It's a good thing I don't answer to you."

"Technically you do," he said as he stood aside when the sheriff came and unlocked her cell door. "Thanks, George." The sheriff nodded and moved off.

"What do you mean?" She hurried to the corridor, unreasonably worried that the sheriff would come back and make her stay.

"My uncle has lived off me for years."

She threw him a doubtful look but knew it quickly turned to panic. If he held the reins to the money, he could...

"Don't worry," he interrupted her thoughts. "I won't fire you, although I may cut your clothing allowance unless you start wearing something less...severe." He finished with a wave at her attire.

"Can we just go, please?" She smelled like a brewery and the soles of her shoes were sticking to the floor. All she could think of was getting a bath and change of clothes, which were becoming scarce, given that two of her suits were now ruined.

She signed for her belongings and exited the building, immediately blinded by the sunlight. "Good Lord, it's morning?" She dug in her purse for her sunglasses, realizing she had left them back in her room.

"Closer to noon," said Jake. He turned in front of her and took off his own sunglasses and gently slid them on her. "Better?"

"I'm not hung over," she pouted as he put a hand to her back to guide her over to his car.

"No," he laughed, "you had time to sleep that off in jail."

She tried to scowl at him, but looking back, it had been an experience she wouldn't soon forget. "Thank you," she said, pushing the too large glasses up her nose. She looked around, not sure where she was. She had only ventured off

Main Street when Lindsay took her out to Jake's cottage, and she realized there was more to the small town than she had known. The street was lined with brick buildings, the painted signs on the windows proclaiming lawyers, a doctor and chiropractor, city hall, and a CPA firm to name a few.

Jake tossed a paper in her lap when she got into the Jeep. "You made the papers," he said and she heard laughter in his voice.

She unfolded the paper to a large photo of the bar fight. Though slightly out of focus, she recognized herself holding a beer bottle aloft. She groaned as she scanned the photo.

"Oh, god," she exclaimed. "Jake, that's you." She pointed to the body on the floor.

Jake shrugged. Shrugged!

"You've been recognized. Now what will you do?"

He grunted as he tried to shift gears with the bandage on his hand. She started to ask him about it, but he shrugged her off. "Read the caption."

She looked back at the paper. "JT Torro Parties Hard on Holiday." She looked up. "Who is JT Torro?"

He looked at her in surprise. "A very well known hard rocker."

"He was at the bar?" she asked.

This made him grin. "No, but the tabloids seem to think so."

She glanced back at the photo. To her, it looked just like Jake, but not Joseph Donovan. If people thought it was Torro, for the time being his identity was safe.

* * *

Jake's hand hurt like a sonofabitch but he had refused the pain pills the island doctor had prescribed. He never took anything stronger than aspirin after seeing what happened to his mother. There were no broken bones, Doc had said and other than some swelling and stiffness, no

67

damage had been done. Aside from the bumps and bruises, Jake felt mighty pleased with himself. Fighting had never been allowed, and while he wouldn't make a habit of it, the whole thing had been cleansing in some way.

All except for the part when he couldn't find Cheyenne after he regained consciousness. Instant panic had set in, and he wouldn't let Cam take him to the clinic until he had assured him Cheyenne was in the custody of the Sheriff and had not been accosted further by that man.

Cam had filled him in on the details while they waited Jake's turn at the clinic.

The sheriff had honed in on Cheyenne and Jake the minute he arrived, and most of the patrons who had been fighting had taken advantage of his preoccupation to slip out the door. It was just as well, Cam had said with a laugh. The island jail only had two small cells. The instigator, Johnny Blaine, was a local fisherman and known not to hold his liquor well. Cam usually refused him more than a beer or two, but with the crowd at the Gold Pelican last night, his count had gotten away from him. He had gotten away, too, but Sheriff Franklin had assured Cam the man would get his due.

Now, as Jake held the Inn door for Cheyenne, he really didn't want to leave her alone. He had thought about taking her back to the cottage, but knew she would want a bath and change of clothes. And she needed sleep. He could do an all nighter when he was composing but knew she wasn't used to the hours he normally kept.

That wasn't the only reason he didn't want to leave, he thought, as he climbed back into the Jeep. She had been spectacular last night. A warrior with a beer bottle, she had no qualms taking on a man three times her size. And she had done so in defense of him. Aside from his mother, there had never been anyone in his life who had stood up for him. His uncle, as his guardian, hadn't cared as much for his welfare as he had for the money he could make. The household staff kept their tongues for fear of their jobs.

But one slip of a woman had been willing to take on all comers; had spent the night in jail; all because of him. He had been the one out of control when he saw Blaine's hands on her. Extreme emotion of the kind he had felt last night was something new and it amazed him.

She had surprised him practically from her first day on the island, or perhaps from the day she had fallen into the bay. She tried so hard to be professional; to do the job assigned her, but he knew that beneath the stiff exterior of Miss Tucker lay a passionate woman. He longed to explore that passion but had a feeling she would be hesitant if he moved too fast. He knew time was running out although the exact number of days left in her timetable eluded him and he was afraid if she left the island without him, he would never see her again.

Music hummed as he parked the Jeep at the cottage. It would seem that he could get neither Cheyenne Tucker nor the music she caused out of his head. He took some aspirin to ease the pain in his hand and sat down at the table where he had left his composition. He had completed the first two movements of the sonata. Revisiting last night's brawl and Cheyenne's monumental actions, he marked out several measures of his current work, changing the tempo. Before he totally lost himself in the music, he set his phone alarm and turned on his keyboard, letting the music flow through him.

Chapter 7

Cheyenne took a last glance in the mirror before heading downstairs when Jake texted that he was waiting. The floral sundress she had purchased fit snuggly across the breast and flared from the waist to end just below her knees. Her heels didn't seem quite appropriate so she settled on sandals. She would have worn her linen slacks and cashmere sweater but after his comment about her clothes, she had decided to dress casually. The bright red, blue and yellow flowers suited her, she thought, as she touched up her lipstick, this time a pale pink shade.

She was glad for the sandals when he insisted they walk. She was happy to be casually dressed when he turned into Brenda Kay's.

"Again?" she asked as they slid into a booth near the back.

"It's rib night," was all he said as Brenda came to the table.

"Well if you don't look a sight," she said as she set water glasses on the table. "Heard there was a ruckus at the Pelican. Damn it, the one night I didn't get down there, but it was too busy for me to get away."

"You didn't miss much," Jake said and Cheyenne coughed.

Brenda looked at her and back to Jake's bandaged hand. "I can see that. How are you going to eat ribs with a broken hand?"

"Carefully," he said with a smile then grimaced and touched his bruised cheek.

Cheyenne was surprised by his good nature. Granted, he hadn't spent the night in jail, but he had been injured and she didn't know if he had gotten any more sleep than she had. He sported his wounds like a banner, almost as though he were proud of the fight he had been in.

She could only shake her head and shrug when Brenda looked back at her.

"Beer?" she asked.

Cheyenne shook her head again. "Not for me. I'll stick with water."

Jake laughed lightly and ordered a soda.

While they waited for their meal, which Cheyenne assumed was ribs whether she had ordered them or not, she studied Jake more closely. The split in his lip looked better, but she could see the fingers on his right hand were slightly swollen. She reached over to lightly touch the scabbed knuckles.

"Does it hurt badly?" She felt so guilty at having caused him injury.

"Cheyenne?" He didn't say any more until she raised her gaze to his. His brown eyes were intense, his smile gentle. "None of this," he gestured with his other hand, "was your fault."

"But I—"

"You were being accosted. Every other man in the bar would have done the same thing. I simply got there first." Irrationally, she heard pride in his voice.

"Your hands are your life, you idiot," she said without thinking, but he only smiled wider.

"You have no idea what I am capable of with only one hand," he whispered across the table and she could feel a blush rising. Honestly, she had never blushed so much in her life until she encountered him.

"Whatever are you thinking, Miss Tucker?" he teased. "I might have simply been implying I was ambidextrous."

She changed the topic instead of bothering to comment. "Tell me what happened after I was hauled off to the slammer."

Their ribs arrived, served up on brown paper as had the fish and chips. The waitress set down a pile of napkins,

71

refilled her water and took Jake's glass to get him another soda. Jake waited until she left before answering her.

"The excitement was over by the time I came to."

She gasped. "You were knocked out completely? Damn it, I told the sheriff to let me see to you, but he hauled me off like a common criminal."

He grinned as he picked up a rib. "Well, actually…"

"You know what I mean." She looked at the pile of ribs, wished for silverware, then with a sigh, picked up the sauce slathered meat and took a bite. A moan of pleasure escaped. They ate in silence for several minutes. When the waitress brought another serving of ribs, Cheyenne looked at her in surprise.

"All you can eat," she replied as she set that down along with Jake's soda.

"One serving *is* all I can eat," she said.

Once again, Jake was silent as he cleaned off rib after rib, licking his fingers in-between bites. By the time he was done, he had barbeque sauce smeared all over his bandage as well as his mouth.

She bit her lower lip as his tongue snaked out to lick sauce off his lips. When he was finished, he sat back with a sigh.

"How did you know where I was?" She picked up their conversation now that he was done.

"It wasn't hard to figure out. You weren't at the Inn and you didn't answer your cell phone. Cam said the sheriff had gotten to you so at least I knew you would be protected from Blaine."

"That was his name?"

He nodded. "Johnny Blaine. I don't know him personally but I hear it's not the first time he's been in trouble. Cam says he takes up jail space more often than not."

"Then he shouldn't be allowed to drink," she said, indignant. "If that had been the case, I wouldn't now have a police record."

He laughed. Was it a good thing that he seemed to laugh quite a bit around her?

72

"Until last night, I bet you've never done one thing that's not strictly by the books," he said.

"I most certainly have," she automatically replied then snapped her mouth shut. He must think she broke the law on a regular basis.

"What; been late for work? I know, you actually called in sick to work but you weren't."

"Of course not. I wouldn't lie about something like that." That didn't mean she hadn't committed other offenses. She thought about the time she stole a box of mac and cheese from the little grocery on the corner in order to feed her and her sister. She had never visited that grocery again; afraid the owner would recognize her.

She sipped her water in contemplation. Surely there was something in her life that would show him she wasn't as straight laced as he thought. She didn't want to think about why that was so important to her.

"There was an incident on my way down here," she said. "I was in the drive-through at Starbucks."

He nodded and smiled. "Of course, a Starbucks, not a McDonalds."

She huffed. "The place is hardly relevant. I was sitting in my car waiting to order and a girl; a woman; jumped out of the passenger side of the car in front of me; yelling. She raced to my car and tried to get in but of course it was locked. She looked behind her where the man driving the car had emerged and was coming after her."

Cheyenne closed her eyes as she remembered the scene. "She was very frightened; yelling something I couldn't understand as he stood by the rear of his car, yelling right back at her. When she realized she couldn't get in my car, she took off and the man started after her."

Her heart pounded even now, thinking about it. "I lifted my foot off the brake and my car rolled forward, just as the man stepped between his car and mine."

Jake's eyes rounded. "You pinned a man between your cars?"

"I couldn't think of anything else to do. That girl was scared out of her wits and it was the only way she could get away."

He lifted his glass in salute. "Well, here's to you."

When she didn't say any more, his eyebrow rose in question. "That can't be the end of the story because you are here, which means you eventually moved out of the Starbuck's line."

She narrowed her gaze, only to have him grin.

"It's not at all funny. He pounded on the hood of my car. Someone in line must have called the police because the minute we heard sirens, he pushed against my car enough to get loose; or maybe I released the pressure on the brakes; I'm not sure. Anyway, he got in his car and sped away."

"And you got your latte and drove happily away."

"I most certainly did not. The police made me pull off to the side and park so I could give them a statement. I was terribly behind schedule by the time they were done. I couldn't take time to go through the whole line again."

"That might have taken what, a day off your schedule? By the way, how many days do you have left?"

"Twenty; and I'm glad you think this is all fun and games, but I have a very real job to do and you are making it extremely difficult."

"Because I won't give in to my uncle who has probably devised a three hundred day worldwide tour to keep me busy and out of trouble?" He scowled. "And to make him more money?"

She had no idea if that were true; Sebastian hadn't given her the particulars of his plans.

"More money is always nice," she said.

"Who needs it? Do you have any idea of my net worth? I'm not bragging; I'm simply saying enough is enough. Money can't buy happiness as they say."

At an earlier time in her life, Cheyenne would have adamantly disagreed with him. When there wasn't enough money to eat; when she had lied about her age to get a job to keep a roof over their heads – yeah, money might not

74

buy happiness but it sure could help keep body and soul together.

As though sensing her mood, Jake changed the subject. "So, getting back to last night. My opinion somewhat changed about you."

Oh, this couldn't be good, Cheyenne thought.

"Not only did you fight dirty, but you used a few choice words on Blaine."

Cheyenne rolled her eyes to the ceiling. "Not exactly what I would want anyone to recall about me."

"That's a good thing," he said, placing his uninjured hand over hers on the table. "You were take-no-prisoners warrior woman, and I was extremely glad you were on my side."

His praise, such as it was, made Cheyenne want to melt into a little puddle at his feet. It was no wonder he had groupies and adoring fans worldwide. And though she refused to be one of the mob because of his music, his soft words and good nature were fast turning her into his biggest admirer. That only made her responsibility to Sebastian Donovan more difficult to fulfill.

"If you think so highly of me, will you please consider my request to return to Chicago?"

He removed his hand from hers. "I am considering it."

She perked up. "Good. There are flights out of Seattle every day."

He shook his head. "Considering is not agreeing. Besides, this weekend is the Mermaid Festival, and I agreed to be on the committee. I can't run out on that."

"They celebrate mermaids?"

"From what I've heard, one of the first families on the island was Able Lockburn and his brothers. They were shrimpers from the mainland, and the legend goes that once they were caught in a fierce storm. Their mast was broken and they were floundering at sea, far from the mainland. All was lost until a mermaid rose from the rolling waves and commanded the seas to calm, then she led them to this island, where they decided to settle."

"Seriously?"

He shrugged. "Who am I to dispute legend? Besides, anything that helps the economy of small islands like Lockabee is cause for celebration. From what I understand, there will be several thousand people here over the two days."

Cheyenne groaned. "This weekend was bad enough. I will have to hide in my room."

He laughed. "Most certainly not, but I'll make sure you have an escort so you don't start any more brawls."

She started to argue but from the twinkle in his eyes realized he was teasing.

"If you wouldn't put yourself in harm's way, I wouldn't have to *brawl*."

He placed a hand over his heart. "You are my hero." He slid out of the booth and stood, back to her, which was a good thing because Cheyenne's breath caught and she knew her face would have given her away. She was falling for Jake Smith. Everything about him in this rustic setting called to her. He was laid back and friendly; good natured and gentlemanly. Yet he fiercely came to her rescue.

She had never been drawn to Joseph Donovan, other than in an awestruck sort of way. That persona had been too far out of her league, whereas Jake Smith was down to earth. She knew it was silly to compare the two when they were the same people, yet it really did seem as if Jake had shaken off the rich and famous cloak. Could someone change so completely in a few short months?

She would have laughed at the thought if it hadn't struck an intimate chord within her. She had done almost the opposite; coming from nothing and building a thin veneer of respectability around herself. She'd worked her way through community college and decided upon graduation that she would never be poor again. She would have the best clothes, the latest phone. She would get her nails done weekly and her hair highlighted regularly. She had managed to become an assistant to one of the world's most famous people and she wasn't about to fail at her assignment.

Jake wondered at her expression as she slid from the booth. He didn't want the professional and efficient mask of Miss Tucker to slide into place when he enjoyed Cheyenne so much more.

"It's early; let's take a walk down to the docks." When she hesitated, he took her hand and tucked it into the crook of his arm. She relaxed and gave him a smile.

As they walked, he tried to think of something to say. He really knew little about her. She had always been in the background of his life; like a shadow doing his uncle's bidding. Now she was constantly in his thoughts.

"It's funny that you have worked for my uncle all these years, yet I really know nothing about you."

"An efficient executive assistant should be inconspicuous."

He gave a bark of laughter. "Do they give you a book in school with a list of rules?"

That made her smile, which made her whole face light up. He wanted to be the one who made her smile all the time.

"Tell me something about yourself."

The smile wavered and he wanted to retract the statement, but she tilted her head slightly and looked at him.

"I have a sister, down in Sweetwater, Texas."

He waited.

"I had a mother, of course, until she…left." The pause was short but he caught her hesitancy. Had her mother died as his had and she was hesitant to mention it?

"Ah, so we have something in common. You didn't mention a father."

"Oh, no. I'm not a bastard," she replied before slapping a hand to her mouth, her eyes widening. "I shouldn't have said…"

"It's not that I haven't been called that; or worse." The fact was, his mother had once told him that she and his father had married, but she had no license and her brother never believed her.

"Still, it's not my place…"

"What exactly is your place, Cheyenne?"

They had reached the top of the pier and stopped. She removed her hand from his arm and folded her arms across the top of the wood railing. She looked off into the distance and the only sounds were the call of the gulls and the gentle slapping of waves against the dock.

He studied her profile. She was pretty; not classically beautiful like the models and dancers who had once been a part of his life. Pretty was better. There was no artifice about her. She was what she was. A very efficient assistant to an imposing man. As such, she was cool and reserved, emotion rarely crossing her face.

At least that was the way he remembered her in Chicago. Since she had tracked him down here on the island, she had become outspoken, tenacious in her quest to get him to return home and fierce in her defense of him in the bar fight. All qualities that made her seductive as hell. He recalled thinking earlier if he weren't hurting so badly, he would take the proper Cheyenne Tucker to bed for a good romp. He wondered which set of emotions would prevail if he put a move on her.

"Forget that question. I don't want to talk about responsibilities. We're merely two ordinary people out on a date."

"Is that even possible?"

He turned toward her and pulled her close. "Let's find out."

He half expected her to resist when he brushed his lips against hers. Instead, she tilted her head and stepped even closer. That answered at least part of his question. Then he wasn't thinking at all as instinct took over. He reached up and plucked the clip from her hair, letting the soft tendrils flow through his fingers as he cupped her face. She smelled of sunshine and roses. Her eyes drifted closed and he kissed her deeply. Immediately the music flowed through him but he wasn't letting go or running off this time. Not when he held a living, breathing symphony in his arms.

She moved against him as he ran his hands down her back, never breaking contact with her luscious lips. He swallowed her soft moan when he pressed her hips against his. He would have done even more had he not been vaguely aware of their surroundings. Slowly, he lifted his mouth, continuing to pepper her face with kisses.

"Come back to the cottage with me," he whispered before tracing the shell of her ear with his tongue.

Her arms loosened from around his neck, her palms sliding down to press lightly against his chest.

"I can't." Even as she said the words, she turned and kissed his cheek.

He leaned back just enough to see her face, keeping her securely in his embrace. "If it's my uncle you're worried about..."

"That's not it," she replied. "There's too much difference between us. You're rich and famous and--"

"Are you after my fortune?" he mockingly glared at her.

"I don't want your money," she cried with very real indignity.

"Good because neither do I." He tightened his hold on her. "It causes nothing but trouble." He didn't let her protest further by covering her lips with his in a kiss that was soft and gentle, yet hopefully told her exactly what he did want.

Chapter 8

This time it was Cheyenne who ran away.

"I have to go," she said, pushing against Jake's chest. Surprisingly, he released her and stood back.

"What are you afraid of, Cheyenne?" His question struck a nerve.

Myself, she thought as she hurried away, leaving him standing by the dock rail alone. She knew if she let Jake close; if they had a relationship, it would devastate her when he ended it. And how could he not? His life was on the stage, and even though he protested now, she knew he would eventually go back to that. He was still composing; he still loved music. It wasn't something anyone with his talent could truly walk away from. And she didn't belong in that world; a place of glamour and parties and hob-knobbing with the rich and famous.

Cheyenne had never considered herself inferior to anyone. In fact, that had been the one thing to keep her going in the darkest days after her mother had left. She had told herself and her sister over and over again that it was their mother who had a problem. They were not the unworthy ones. That attitude had made it possible to do the impossible at the time – to become an adult when she was still a child in order to keep them from being separated and going into the system.

So why did she feel she wasn't good enough for Jake? Because he was actually Joseph Donovan, she reminded herself as she readied for bed. She knew he'd had affairs with glamorous women. She had frequently seen the photos in the tabloids; in fact, she had often issued press releases written by the senior Donovan disputing any stories and liaisons that had been printed.

She crawled into bed without checking her phone or email. Her mind was in turmoil over a situation she hadn't wanted in the beginning and now was being swept into the storm. If only Sebastian had sent someone else to collect Jake; if only she hadn't kissed him that first time; if only her brain would quit wondering what it would be like to make love with him.

She eventually fell asleep, dreaming of belonging to someone and living a life of happily ever after.

* * *

Cheyenne looked blurrily at the readout on her phone.
Be outside in an hour. Dress casual.

Well, he wasn't giving up, she thought, as she dragged herself to the shower. A smile curved her lips as she stood under the spray. *He wasn't giving up.*

She dressed in navy Bermuda shorts and a red and white crop top, pulled her hair back in a pony tail and applied light make up. She wished she had tennis shoes, but her deck shoes would have to do. Honestly, if she ended up spending the rest of the month here, she had to get more clothes. Jake no longer evaded her, but he certainly hadn't consented to returning to Chicago, which meant she was here for the duration.

Feeling slightly guilty, she fired off a quick email to Donovan, telling him she had information and would get back to him as soon as she could. It wasn't exactly a lie, but she had come to the conclusion that this really wasn't her fight. Jake was an adult, certainly capable of deciding his life. His uncle needed to understand that, but it wasn't her place to tell him so. After what Jake had told her about his mother, she was leaning more heavily in his favor, even though she was employed by the opposition.

She hurried down the stairs, grabbed a bottle of water and a French pastry from the breakfast tray, and left all thoughts of Chicago behind as she closed the door.

The heat assaulted her; the sun already bouncing off the light colored walls of the buildings. She did have her sunglasses, which she hastily donned, but could have used a hat.

Jake stood at the bottom of the steps. He wore ragged cutoffs, a tee with the sleeves torn off and tennis shoes with a hole in one toe. His ball cap was turned backwards, his mirrored sunglasses reflecting the bright light.

"You have only been here two months," she said as she joined him and they started down the boardwalk. "How is it your clothes look like they survived every natural disaster known to man?"

He laughed and she was glad to see he harbored no ill feelings for her having run out on him last night. "You can actually buy clothes this way."

"The question is, why would you want to?"

"You need a hat," he said instead. He grabbed her hand and led her into a souvenir shop.

She took a step toward the wide brimmed sun hats but he pulled her the opposite way.

"You'll need something that stays on your head." He grabbed one from the shelf. It had a fish coming out of water with a huge hook in its mouth. Embroidered in hot pink on the black material was *"hook'er"*.

"Seriously?" she choked out but had to laugh when he turned back around and she saw the front of his hat. *"Chick bait"* was scrawled next to a can of worms.

"Is there anything that doesn't have to do with fish and sex?" she asked.

He looked at her with mock surprise. "This entire island is supported by fishing."

"And the sex?" she questioned without thinking.

He wiggled his brows as he plucked another hat from a lower shelf. "How do you think they make the next generation of fishermen?" He started to put the white hat on her head, then reached behind her and pulled her pony tail out through the hole in the back.

"What does this one say?" She tried to pull it off but he caught her hand and held it tight. She noticed he had replaced his bandage with a brace that wrapped around his wrist and palm, leaving his fingers free. She momentarily forgot about the hat as she studied his hand, assuring herself the swelling had gone down.

He kept hold of her as he gave the cashier some money.

"Fitting." The man nodded toward her hat as he handed Jake his change. "And not just because of the festival."

Cheyenne pulled her hand free and sought a mirror. She wasn't leaving this store with a derogatory saying on her hat. It took her a minute to read the word backward, then she smiled as Jake came up behind her. *"Mermaid"* was stenciled in emerald green, arching around a picture of the aforesaid, her long blonde hair barely covering lush breasts.

He smiled at her reflection in the mirror and she mentally took back her earlier thoughts about wishing Donovan hadn't given her this assignment. At the moment, there was nowhere else she would rather be.

The street had become more crowded during their time in the store and Jake grabbed her hand to keep them together. "We're heading for the pier," he said as they wove in and out of the crowds.

"The festival has already started?" There weren't as many people clogging the streets as on Magnificent Mile for the Christmas parade, but for a small village, it seemed overwhelming.

"The official kickoff is at sunset, which is why we need to hustle." He quickened his pace and she easily kept up with his long stride. At the pier, they veered off the boardwalk onto one of the floating docks, lined with boats on both sides. This particular dock jutted the farthest out into the harbor, and they walked almost to the end where a boat was tied in the last slip.

"Sorry for the delay, McNally," Jake said as he hopped aboard then turned to help her. Instead of giving her a hand, he circled her waist and lifted her across. She grabbed his upper arms in reflex. He was muscular but not bulky and his skin was warm beneath her fingers. She reluctantly let go when her feet hit the deck but grabbed him again when her shoes slipped on the wet surface.

He kept one hand circled about her upper arm. "Take off the shoes," he said, helping her to maintain her balance as she pulled one then the other off and dropped them on the deck.

He then turned to introduce her to the other man. "McNally, this is Cheyenne Tucker, a friend. Thought she might like to see what we're up to." To her he added, "McNally is the unofficial harbormaster."

McNally, a barrel chested man with a red beard and bright blue eyes, grinned at her as he tugged the front of his hat. "Welcome aboard, Miss. You both sit back there while I get us under way."

Cheyenne moved in the direction he indicated, sitting down on a cushion bench along the back of the boat. McNally climbed the few steps to an area where he apparently captained the boat and Jake slipped the tether free of the cleat.

"Are you okay?" he asked as he sat beside her, toeing off his own shoes and kicking them aside. "You don't get seasick, do you?" He tilted his head to look at her with a frown.

"Of course not," she instantly replied, hoping it was true. She had taken the Chicago River cruises, and once a coastline boat tour on Lake Michigan but both were different from going out to sea, if that was where they were heading.

As though reading her thoughts, he said, "We're not going beyond the harbor buoys." He pointed to a spot beyond them and Cheyenne could see orange balls bobbing on the water's surface. He pulled a box between his feet to rummage through then handed her a stack of numbered oil cloth flags with riveted holes on two corners.

"Our job is to give each boat a number if they want to be in the flotilla tonight. I'll cut lengths of rope and you can thread them through the holes. They'll tie these to their main sail mast so we know they registered."

"What exactly is a flotilla?" she asked as they worked. Occasionally his warm shoulder bumped hers and butterflies kicked up in her stomach. At least she told herself that, as she didn't want to get seasick in front of him.

"Boats from Lockabee and other nearby islands sail and motor over, forming an armada across the harbor and around the island. The boats string lights all over, tie closely together stem to stern, and basically party. From what I hear, it's quite the event, and with little moon, the lights should be spectacular."

Cheyenne fell silent, watching Jake as he worked. His feet were lean and brown as was the rest of his body that she could see. *Thinking about his body is not what you should be doing,* she chastised herself. Instead, she thought how Jake had made himself part of this small community. He knew residents and was friendly and helpful, not at all reserved and stand-offish as he had been in Chicago. As the boat bounced across the water to the first boat in the area, she wondered what it would be like to belong somewhere. They had moved around a lot growing up because whenever her mom couldn't pay the rent, they would get evicted and she would simply pile them in the old car and roll down the road to another small town where she could get a room, or until they ran out of gas.

Shaking off old memories, she concentrated on the task before her. One by one, McNally sidled up to the boats and Jake passed over the flags, collecting a small registration fee he said would help offset the cost of fireworks that would be shot off from a barge Sunday evening.

"Better put on some sunscreen," McNally said at one point, tossing her a tub of lotion. "You must be a tourist with that pale skin."

Jake grinned and offered to do her legs. She ignored his comment, but stood and lifted her foot to the bench beside him, rubbing the cream up her calf and over her thigh. She heard a groan and wondered at the pained expression on his face before he got up and headed down to the galley for water. He came back with three bottles, passed one to McNally and rubbed one across his brow as he sat beside her again.

"Drink," he said as he opened her bottle and gave it to her. "Regardless of the water all around us, it's easy to get dehydrated in the sun."

Every time she thought they were done, another boat appeared, tossing an anchor into the shallow harbor. The boats were all sizes from small two sail cutters to larger yachts and pontoons. Everyone was friendly, offering them drinks as they floated by. It would seem this was the summer party not to be missed. The sun beat down, the temperature rose and Cheyenne found herself sweating. She wiped an arm across her brow.

As they headed back to the pier, Jake went up and spoke softly to the man at the wheel. He came back to where she sat, hands on hips, and grinned at her. "Can you swim?"

"Of course I can swim."

"Very well?" His smile was growing and she suddenly had a suspicion of what he was up to.

She glanced toward the pier and the sandy beach which lay to the side. Colorful umbrellas and beach towels dotted the surface and people were everywhere. That was her mistake, for the minute her back was turned, Jake caught her beneath the arms and legs and stepped onto the cushioned seat. She grabbed him around the neck.

"Don't you dare!" She squealed just before McNally cut the motor and Jake jumped.

Water rushed over her and she came up sputtering. Jake reached for her but she knocked his arm aside and cupped her hands, pushing a wave of water over his face. Before he could catch her, she pushed him under. If he wanted to play, she could hold her own.

He grabbed her leg and pulled her under with him, tugging her close until every inch of her felt every inch of him. He locked his lips to hers and shared his breath and for endless moments they floated in the crystal clear water. When they surfaced, McNally was leaning over the back of the boat.

"Thought maybe the sharks got you," he said.

Cheyenne swiveled her head in all directions, panic causing her heart to skip a beat.

She paddled a few strokes to the boat where she grabbed a hand rail. Jake swam up beside her. "There are no sharks this close," he said. "Dolphins, maybe."

She pushed her drooping hat back from her forehead and tried to glare but the water actually felt good. It had cooled her off but now the thought of Jake's kiss only heated her back up.

McNally took her hand and pulled her out of the water. Just as Jake pulled himself up, she turned and pushed him back in.

"You have ruined almost all my clothes," she started, but he only laughed.

"I'll buy you more," he said, treading water. "And maybe a bikini."

The idea of him seeing her in a swim suit, much less a bikini, had water droplets sizzling off her overheated skin. "You are certifiable."

"All the more reason for you to stay very close to me." He lowered his voice. "You wouldn't want me to do something disgraceful to the Donovan name." He back paddled a few strokes, his gaze still intent on her. "That means you have to swim to shore with me."

Cheyenne glanced up, gauging the distance. It couldn't be more than fifty yards, a doable distance. "You're serious?"

"Come on. It shouldn't be hard for a mermaid." She touched her hat, the one he had bought her. No one ever bought her gifts, even sensible things like hats and clothes. Since she didn't want to lose it, she climbed onto the back of the boat and slid into the water feet first, keeping her head above water.

He set a leisurely pace and she easily kept up with him doing the breast stroke.

"When did you learn to swim?" she asked, thinking of what he had told her about his strict education.

"Oh, Uncle made sure I learned but not for pleasure. He said if I should be on some rich patron's yacht and something went wrong, I needed to be able to save myself."

Cheyenne was beginning to think less of the senior Donovan. "Did you learn to jump out of a plane for the same reason?"

That made him laugh. "I'm sure I would have if he had thought of it."

Cheyenne jerked her foot up when something brushed against her but realized it was the sandy bottom as Jake stood up. She got her feet beneath her and together they waded to shore, him pulling her by the hand. No one even bothered to look their way, for which she was glad considering the way her shirt clung to her skin, her bra visible beneath the thin material.

"That was…refreshing," she said when they stopped at the edge of the beach. "Although I probably look a sight."

"You look," he started but paused.

"Like a drowned cat?" She arched a brow.

"I was going to say pretty," he started and she scoffed. "Really; you are, but I think the word I want is normal." He straightened her hat.

She knew her gaze reflected her confusion, but honestly, "What kind of a statement is that?"

"It's hard to explain," he said with a shrug. "You're Cheyenne, not Miss Tucker."

Though it sounded strange, she understood because she had seen the same changes in him. Here on Lockabee, he was Jake Smith, not the famous Joseph Donovan. And she had to admit she liked the casual, relaxed atmosphere of the small village where she didn't have to worry that someone would see through her and discover she wasn't as prim and proper as her job required. That she liked a good joke and a cold beer.

"Come on," he said, shrugging off the introspection. "The sand will be hot, but if we walk in the shallows closer to the pier, there won't be as much to worry about."

They managed the sand in a few hops and Jake led her weaving around the people and dock ropes until they were once again at McNally's boat.

"So you didn't drown him," the older man commented as he handed over their shoes.

"It was a very near thing," she replied with a laugh. She laughed harder when Jake grabbed her and swung her out over the water again.

"We'd better go," he said, shaking McNally's hand. "Thanks for the escort today."

"Anytime," he replied then winked at Cheyenne. "You keep him in line now."

She blushed at the thought this man considered her and Jake a couple.

"I'm starved," Jake said as they exited the pier and moved along the boardwalk. "Let's eat."

She looked down at her drying but now salt-crusty clothes. "I can't go anywhere like this. I'm beginning to itch from the salt."

"This'll work," Jake said, ignoring her as he stopped at a food vendor on the corner. He dug some soggy bills out of his pocket and soon they were eating fish po'boys as they walked along. The fish was fresh and crisp and the sauce tangy on her tongue. She even ate every last crumb of the crusty roll. At least the swim today had worked off a few calories.

"Jake! Jake!" A female voice calling his name had them both turning around. Brenda Kay was heading their way and from the look on her face, in a panic.

"What's up?"

"I need help. Mary Beth called in sick, though I'm sure she's off somewhere with her boyfriend enjoying the festival. Bonnie's daughter went into labor and so I'm cooking and trying to wait tables."

"What about Lindsay?" Cheyenne asked, thinking of the one person she knew on the island.

"Are you kidding? She makes more on a single ride than I can pay for the day," the woman said.

Jake looked at her then back at Brenda Kay. "I was going to show Cheyenne around, but give me thirty minutes to get some fresh clothes and I'll help you out."

Cheyenne watched in amazement as Brenda reached up with both hands on his cheeks and kissed him squarely on the mouth.

"You're a doll! Can you make it in twenty?" Then she was gone.

"Okay," Jake drew the word out as they turned and hurried along the boardwalk. "So much for the rest of my plans." He saw her to the door of the Inn. "I'll call when I can get away, but it might be awhile before I see you."

Not as long as you think, Cheyenne thought as she hurried inside.

* * *

Jake made it back to the restaurant in less than half an hour, but stopped short just inside the door. Standing beside the table to his right, Cheyenne chatted with a foursome as she took their orders. She wore a bright pink top and white shorts with a checkered apron tied around her waist. She stuck her pencil in her bun, pad in her pocket and walked to the kitchen window where she put her order on the turn-clip.

He was fascinated by yet another side of her. Gone was the proper executive assistant, although she was definitely still efficient as she bussed a table while she waited for her order. She was perfectly at ease as a waitress, and he watched as she gathered four glasses of water and took them to another table just filling up.

"You going to gawk or did you come to help?" Brenda Kay asked as she hurried by.

"Don't complain about free help," he countered. "Where do you want me?"

She laughed out loud. "Honey, that is such a loaded question. I'm sure your lady friend would know the answer."

He glanced over to where Cheyenne bustled from table to table, refilling water and handing out napkins. His groin tightened and he wondered if the few kisses they had shared could indeed lead to something more. Brenda Kay's smack to his chest, apron in hand, quickly scattered his daydreams.

For the next several hours, he had no opportunity to talk to Cheyenne as they busted their butts with tourist traffic. She gave him a quick "hey" when they met at the window putting up orders, but had no more time when someone from her section called her over.

Jake wasn't nearly as efficient as she and Becky, the other waitress, and more than once took an order to the wrong table. No one seemed to mind, and orders were quickly replaced with correct ones, but for probably the first time in his life, he didn't excel at a job. Surprisingly, it didn't bother him and he grinned as his apron pocket jingled with tips as the night wore on.

There was a lull after the dinner hour ended at eight, and Brenda Kay brought out some fresh fish and chips. "Eat while you can," she said. "We'll get another rush after the music at the park." They all sat down gratefully at a back table and ate without talking.

When Brenda and Becky went back to the kitchen, Jake put a hand out as Cheyenne also started to rise. "Sit for another minute."

She did as he asked, but he noticed she looked everywhere but at him. "Hey." He turned her to face him with a finger to her chin. "What's up?"

"I'm sorry. Brenda asked for your help and I butted in, but she seemed so desperate."

"Jeez, don't apologize. You are fantastic. For me it's been like an orchestra warming up. Everyone is playing their own little piece; nothing meshes so the notes are discordant and the beat is off. I don't see how you keep it all straight."

She gave him a tired smile. "The first time I ever saw you, it was at the Oriole with your uncle. I had no idea who either of you were at the time. I was your waitress and he

91

had a terrible tantrum because the meat was not as tender as he liked. He actually got up and threw it in the trash."

"My uncle tends to be ...flamboyant."

"That may be, but for someone working her way through school and not always knowing where her next meal will come from, it was beyond wasteful." She blushed slightly. "I'm afraid I told him so."

"I don't remember that. I would think I'd remember something that impressive."

"Well, I'm certainly glad he didn't remember a year later when I applied for a job at the Academy. I nearly dropped through the floor when I went into his office for an interview and recognized him."

Her statements gave him more insight into her background and personality than she probably would have liked. From the sounds of it, she came from a poor background but had managed to overcome it. She now had sophistication and polish but was severe in self-discipline and efficiency from her bun to her four-inch heels. That was how she had appeared the first time he saw her on the island. Now she enthusiastically roughhoused with him in the harbor and unabashedly waited on tables in shorts and a tank. He didn't even want to think about the kisses they had shared.

It was like she was two different people, he thought, as she left him to greet new arrivals. There were hidden depths to Cheyenne Tucker and he intended to unearth all her secrets.

Chapter 9

It had been a long time since Cheyenne had spent so many hours on her feet and by the time Brenda Kay closed the restaurant doors at 11:30, she longed only for her bed. She twisted the cap on the last of the condiment bottles she had refilled, placed it on the tray with the others and turned toward the kitchen to put them in the refrigerator.

"Ack!" Jake was right behind her. The bottles wobbled and tipped but he grabbed the tray and steadied it.

"I'll take that," he said, easily balancing the tray. "You look beat. Sit for a minute and I'll be right back." He turned for the kitchen.

Cheyenne reached up and pulled the clip from her hair, running her fingers through the long strands. If he thought she looked beat, that couldn't be good. While he had praised her for helping out, she now realized she wanted more from him, and looking like a wilted flower wasn't going to get it.

Brenda Kay came over. "Here's your pay for the night," she said, holding out several bills.

Cheyenne shook her head. "You don't need to pay me. I was just helping out." She dug in her pocket. "In fact, you can have my tip money, too." She dumped a handful of coins and bills onto the table.

"Mine, too," Jake said from behind her. "Although I doubt I have as much as Cheyenne. She was definitely the star waitress tonight."

She blushed at his praise.

Brenda Kay looked from one to the other as a slow smile creased her face. "You two should take that and go have a nice dinner somewhere."

"This is a nice place for dinner," Cheyenne stated emphatically just as Jake said, "I can afford dinner."

The older lady laughed. "Get out of here. There's probably still partying going on."

Before she could protest, Jake grabbed her hand and pulled her out into the street. Music still wafted across the breeze, and lights along Main Street were bright enough for one to think it was midday instead of midnight.

"Do you feel like walking down to the pier to see the flotilla?" Jake had moved his arm to her shoulders, holding her close.

Cheyenne's feet hurt, her back ached, and she was sure she smelled like fryer grease. "Why not? I had nothing else planned for the middle of the night."

He gave her shoulders a squeeze as he laughed. They stopped at one of the vendors along the way and he purchased a couple of bottles of water before leading her down the pier to where McNally's boat had been earlier. The pier security lights didn't reach quite this far, and the soft night closed around them.

"He's no doubt trolling the flotilla," Jake said as he pulled her down so their feet dangled off the end of the pier.

"Keeping everyone in line?" she asked.

"No. Probably partying along with the rest of them." He laughed.

Cheyenne looked out over the glassy water and sucked in a breath. Hundreds, probably thousands of lights flickered across the harbor. Though most were white, every so often a boat was silhouetted in blue and red; green or purple. She glanced to the right where the lights appeared to stretch into infinity. When she turned her head to the left, she encountered Jake's lips, close but not quite touching.

"It's beautiful," she whispered, afraid to break the spell.

"You're beautiful," he corrected, and then there was only the sound of lapping water as his lips took hers. As always, his kiss started out gentle, his lips a feathery caress of her own. She fumbled to set her bottle aside so she could circle his waist. The moment she did, all she could do was hold on for dear life as he deepened the kiss and took her soaring. He pulled her close until their chests touched and their hearts beat as one.

She clutched at his shirt, wanting to feel his skin. Deciding that sitting sideways to him in an embrace wasn't enough, she leaned back and he followed her down so he was laying half over her. His weight felt wonderful and she groaned when he shifted to the side.

"I'm too heavy for you," he whispered as he rained kisses along her jaw and down her throat.

"No," she protested, but when his hand slid beneath her top and touched her bare stomach, her brain shut down. Hands she had watched brilliantly play a piano caressed her in the same manner; lightly sliding and teasing, never stopping long at any one spot. The pads of his fingers were slightly calloused, which only heightened the sensations on her skin. She jerked at his shirt, pulling it up so she could share the pleasure of touch.

The minute she touched his bare back, his skin twitched and he groaned. He reached up with one hand and jerked his shirt over his head, stuffing it beneath her head as a cushion. He was warm to the touch, his muscles bunching and relaxing as she massaged his back.

"That feels good," he breathed the words against her ear as he nibbled on her lobe.

"My sister used to give me a back rub after work," she remembered. "It always helped."

"Then allow me the pleasure," he said. Without releasing her, he rolled slightly to the side so his hands could reach her back. Instead of massaging, he unhooked her bra.

"Jake," she said cautiously.

"Sh, I can't do a proper job with all that in the way."

95

It had been a token protest at best, for she wanted him to touch her everywhere. In the quiet night with the water as accompaniment, she was but an ordinary girl, yet he was still extraordinary; his hands and mouth caressing everywhere until all her nerves were alive. When he nudged her blouse up and sucked her breast into his hot mouth, her back bowed and she cried out from the exquisite pleasure that lanced through her.

Jake gloried in her immediate response to him. She made him feel alive for the first time in months, feelings he had buried now bursting to life. His palm rubbed the tip of her breast and it pebbled beneath his touch. He sucked the other harder to illicit another groan from her. His tongue slid over the plump mound and teased the tender underside as she wiggled beneath him.

He fumbled at the waist of her shorts, found the button and pulled down the zipper. When she offered no resistance, he slid his hand over her lower abdomen to her curls. Their groans simultaneously filled the air. Delving deeper, he found her wet and hot and slid a finger into her. She pulled on his hair but he refused to stop, sliding again and again across the sensitive nub of her pleasure.

She tugged harder, and he released her breast to reclaim her mouth, silencing any protest she might have made. Her arms tightened around his neck as his tongue dipped inside her mouth to fully taste her and his fingers played her until she was wreathing beneath him. She bumped against him, and as though sensing his need, brought her knee up until her thigh rubbed against his throbbing erection. Barely aware of where they were, he knew the improbability of making love to her at that moment, but he could at least finish what he had started.

He pressed the heel of his hand against her nub and slid another finger deeply into her. She arched, tearing her mouth from his to cry out, the sounds whipped away by the breeze. Together they rode the waves of her convulsions. When he tried to remove his hand, she clutched her thighs so he cupped her mound and felt the last of the quivers course through her. With a sigh, she relaxed, tucking her face against his shoulder and he held her lightly.

Once, he would have never thought he could feel this deeply. His life had seemed shallow; living to perform and to please his uncle. He had finally realized he could never meet that standard. Yet he kept trying to find the illusive something that was missing from his life; the wonder that had always made his mother smile when he was with her.

He was beginning to understand what that might be. He bent down to kiss Cheyenne's forehead, whispering softly. "I think I may be in love with you." God only knew what she would have to say about that, he thought ruefully, given her sometimes prickly nature. She stirred in his arms and he decided for now, that realization was for him alone.

Cheyenne slowly opened her eyes but didn't move from the warmth of Jake's embrace. She couldn't believe she had fallen asleep after what had happened. Indeed, she thought perhaps she had passed out after coming so completely apart in his arms. Either way, she nuzzled his shoulder, wondering how long she could pretend to be asleep. She wasn't sure how to act, especially considering what she still felt against her thigh. Her orgasm had sent her over the moon, but he was still hard as stone. She slid her hand down to touch the ridged line of his shorts.

His hand grabbed her wrist. "Don't." His voice wasn't mad, but he did sound a little desperate.

"But you didn't—"

"Tonight was for you," he said, kissing her nose when she looked up at him. He gently cupped her cheek and his look was so adoring, she almost gasped. What was he thinking to look at her like that?

"Jake, we…" She wasn't sure what she wanted to say, but apparently he didn't need the words.

"Next time," he said as he held out a hand and pulled her to her feet. She quickly tugged up her shorts but when she reached around to hook her bra, his hands met hers. "Allow me." He smiled as he deftly fastened her.

"You have very quick hands."

He stepped back and held his hands up, looking from one to the other. "I have amazing hands," he said in all seriousness as he wiggled his fingers.

She laughed at his silliness and all the awkwardness disappeared. They walked back up the pier and down the nearly deserted street arm in arm. He kissed her lightly at the door of the Inn.

"Get some sleep," he said softly as he disappeared into the night but all Cheyenne recalled as she readied for bed was…

"Next time."

* * *

Jake's situation was still apparent when he reached the cottage and he knew even a cold shower wouldn't help, so he poured himself into his music. His pencil flew across the composition paper, the notes appearing out of nowhere to fill page after page. He didn't need to play the music for her moans of pleasure still rang in his ears and the sweet scent of her clung to his skin. He knew this would be his best piece ever, but it certainly wasn't for his uncle. The music before him, from his heart, was meant for only one person, but he would have to find a way to make her accept what they shared.

He knew she would not hesitate to come to his bed when the time came; not after what they had experienced tonight. But he wanted much more from Miss Cheyenne Tucker than a few nights of bliss. He would have to overcome her resistance, and he knew that couldn't be done by showering her with his wealth. She had to be the only woman in a million who thumbed her nose at money unless she had earned it herself. And even then, she was generous with what she had, as she evidenced tonight when she refused to take any wages from Brenda Kay.

He finally fell into bed exhausted, his dreams full of creamy softness, lush breasts and cries of passion. He would have slept the day away had not his phone awakened him. When he didn't reach it in time, it immediately started ringing again. He rubbed a hand over his stubbly chin as he punched speaker so he could start his coffee but instead of filling the coffee pot, he ducked his head under the faucet trying to clear it of sleep.

"'Lo," he bubbled.

"You swimming?" George Franklin's voice boomed across the line. Jake quickly grabbed a hand towel and dried himself.

"What's up, Sheriff? Please don't tell me Miss Tucker is back in custody. It's only eleven in the morning."

The Sheriff laughed. "I need help, Jake, and you're the only one I can think of."

Jake groaned at the thought of doing crowd control and said as much.

"That might be easier," replied the man. "Why the hell she had to plan a wedding for the same weekend as a damned festival, I'll never know, but now we have no piano player and she's in tears and her mother says I'd better come up with one or else."

Jake shook his head to clear it. "Whose wedding?"

"My daughter, Ramsey."

"Well, congratulations." Jake wasn't sure what else to say, as the man didn't sound at all excited. "That sounds like a grand affair."

"It will be if you consent to play at the wedding."

Jake had no trouble helping the sheriff, especially when he had kept Cheyenne's and his names off the record after the bar fight. "Sure, I can do that. When is the wedding?"

"Today at three at the community church. Thanks, kiddo." The call disconnected and Jake was left staring at his phone, wondering what had just happened. There went his plans to escort Cheyenne around the festival, he thought as he finally started the coffee. Between McNally, Brenda Kay and now the sheriff, it was hard getting any time alone with her. And now that he had tasted the wonder of her, he couldn't wait for another chance to make her his.

He punched in her number and when she answered, he blurted out, "Want to go to a wedding today?"

"What?" she squawked.

He realized how that had sounded and laughed. "Not mine, for Pete's sake. The sheriff's daughter is getting married, and apparently they suddenly don't have a pianist."

"Oh," she sounded relieved. "Are you sure you should do that, being in cognito and everything?"

"Playing for a wedding in this community wouldn't be like playing a Grand piano at Carnegie."

"Maybe, but you'll be up front just like on a stage." She sounded awfully worried.

"Look at it this way. If someone recognizes me and word gets out, you'll be absolved of responsibility for telling my uncle."

"That's not even funny," she retorted. "I'm not ready…you're not ready to go home."

Jake caught her slip and smiled. Ah, sweet Cheyenne was overcoming Miss Tucker.

"Come with me," he pleaded.

"Both my suits have been ruined, if you recall. Although Mrs. Godfrey sent them to the mainland cleaners with some of the linens, they're not back yet. I have nothing to wear."

"That will work," he teased.

"You're impossible."

"Cheyenne, please." Had he ever begged for a woman's attention before? He frowned at the thought until he realized that for this particular woman, he would get down on his knees. The very idea surprised him and yet he knew it was true.

"What time?"

"I need to be there at 2:30 to play as people come in."

"What about the music? Surely you don't have Wagner's *Wedding March* tucked away in that cottage."

"Have you forgotten who I am?"

"Oh, right. Pick me up?"

"Two o'clock," he replied and hung up. The smile never left his lips as he dug through the small closet looking for something to wear. Regardless of what she said, Cheyenne was beginning to see him as Jake Smith, not Joseph Donovan. One barrier down, but who knew how many more she would erect before giving in to the inevitable.

* * *

"You look nice," she said as Jake held the Jeep door for her. He was impeccably dressed in a light blue shirt and print tie with black trousers, his black loafers buffed to a high shine. She had wondered if he had anything better to wear than his cargo shorts and polo shirt. Her voice must have given her thoughts away because he raised a brow at her comment and she blushed.

"And you look lovely," he said. "Much better than in those starchy suits."

She sputtered but he laughed and she realized he teased her. She was still getting used to the huge differences between Jake as she knew him now and the man he had left behind in Chicago.

She gathered in the side of her dress so he could close the door. She had settled on her sundress, but wore heels this time instead of sandals. She had left her hair down, letting it curl about her shoulders.

When he settled in the driver's seat, he turned toward her and reached across the distance to curl his hand behind her neck. Tugging her closer, he kissed her, then turned back to start the engine.

"You'll mess my lipstick," she said, even as she licked her lips where his taste lingered.

His gaze narrowed. "I'd like to mess up a whole lot more of you."

When? Her brain hollered. She pinched her lips together to keep from saying the word out loud.

He left her outside as soon as they arrived at the church, excusing himself with yet another quick kiss. Cheyenne thought she could get very used to his kisses.

"My, my, look at you." The voice, full of laughter, came from behind her and she turned to see Lindsay brake to a stop.

"Hello, there." She swished her hips. "Thanks again for the fashion advice."

"Ha! That's not what I was talking about and you know it." She stepped off her bike and Cheyenne noticed for the first time the decorations draped along the back edges of the rickshaw.

It was a good way to change the topic.

"You're all decked out, and not just the rickshaw." Lindsay wore white Bermuda shorts and a pale blue top. Instead of her perpetual ball cap, her hair was piled on top her head in curls.

"I'm the official bridal transportation," she said. "After the ceremony, I'll take them on a loop downtown so everyone can gawk before depositing them at the reception." She looked around as people began arriving. Soft music filtered out the open doors of the church. "That doesn't sound like the regular pianist."

Cheyenne instantly recognized one of Donovan's classics, *Summer Love*, from the last album he had released. She panicked thinking that others may recognize it as well, and in turn see through his guise. Why wasn't he playing someone else's songs?

"Looks like the whole town has turned out, even in the midst of the festival," Lindsay commented as they made their way into the small church. "But with the carnival over at West Bay, most of the tourist crowd will be there all day."

"West Bay?" Cheyenne asked as they took seats near the back of the church.

Lindsay leaned closer. "Down on the southwest part of the island. Not as inhabited as Princetown so there's lots of room for people to spread out. It's like a state fair without the livestock exhibits. Then tonight is a huge concert, so

102

unless you're into drunken half naked groupies, I'd stay away."

"Groupies?"

Lindsay shrugged. "Some hard rock groups I've never heard of. I'm more into whatever that pianist is playing." She closed her eyes and swayed slightly with the music.

Cheyenne's head snapped to the front of the church, but she couldn't see Jake. The altar was covered with flowers, which was probably a good thing. Regardless of his long, sun bleached hair, Jake had a presence about him when he performed that would be difficult to hide.

At that moment, the minister walked out of a side door, followed by two young men Cheyenne could only guess were the groom and best man. The minute they were in place, the music rose to a crescendo and Wagner's *Wedding March* began. Shivers raced down her back as the powerful music filled the small sanctuary. As she stood and turned toward the back, her awareness wasn't for the familiar wedding processional but for the man behind the sound because she knew exactly how those musical fingers felt against her skin. She clutched the back of the pew as a wave of longing swept through her.

"You okay?" Lindsay whispered.

She nodded, giving her a weak smile. Her heart didn't slow until the music softened, then stopped as the ceremony began.

The bride was beautiful, as all brides are, and as Cheyenne watched them, she felt another sense of longing. Would she ever find a love like she could see on the faces of the two young people at the front of the congregation? Did she even want that? She worried that she couldn't make a commitment; that maybe she had too much of her mother's flightiness. Was that why, although she longed for Jake's touch, she knew from the start it wasn't a relationship that would last?

The music started again, and Cheyenne automatically stood with the rest of the guests. The recessional was *You Are the Sunshine of My Life* and she wondered if it had been the bride's pick, or Jake's. Regardless, it certainly fit as the bride and groom, with eyes only for each other, hurried down the aisle.

"I have to go," Lindsay said. "Maybe I'll see you later at the reception?"

"Oh, I don't know," Cheyenne started. Jake hadn't said anything about staying for the reception. Would he have to play there, too?

Lindsay hurried away and Cheyenne made her way out of the church along with the other guests. She wasn't sure what to do, or where she would find Jake, but Brenda Kay was suddenly at her side, pulling her along.

"We have to form the wedding corridor," she said, giving Cheyenne a very long unlit sparkler. "Stay here beside me. When the bride and groom are ready to depart, the sparklers will be lit and held aloft as they pass by." She pointed to the far end of the line of people where Cheyenne could see Lindsay pulling her decorated rickshaw into position.

She was soon caught up in the enthusiasm of the crowd, and hollered along with the rest, waving her sparkler, as the happy couple passed. When it was over and people began leaving, she looked around for Jake. He stood at the top of the church steps, hands in his front pockets, a thoughtful expression on his face. She took a step toward him and as she came into his view, he brightened, smiling as he came down the steps and caught her in a hug.

"Great wedding."

"Great music," she replied.

He kept one arm around her waist and started walking. "I can manage a decent tune now and then."

"Uh-huh. Just now and then?" She tucked her arm behind his back and they followed the crowd to the Community Center behind the church where the reception was already in full swing.

Jake didn't give Cheyenne a chance to get away as he swung her right into the dancing crowd. The DJ was playing a slow dance and he pulled her close, tucking her head in the crook of his neck and wrapping both arms around her. The wedding and the traditional music he had played had left him melancholy. Could he ever find a love like that? Did his profession and the celebrity status naturally attached to it prevent him from finding someone who could love him for himself? Was that yet another reason he had turned away from fame and fortune?

A faint whiff of perfume made him smile as he remembered last night and how Cheyenne had fallen apart in his arms. He spun her into a turn and she lifted her head with a laugh. Her eyes sparkled and he bent to kiss her. Perhaps he was lucky enough to have already found what he was seeking.

Chapter 10

They danced for hours; the DJ doing a credible job of switching the music between fast and slow, current and past tunes. She didn't always partner with Jake for he was in high demand. She enjoyed watching him when she sat on the sidelines, for he bestowed his smile on young and old alike. At the end of a dance with the tiny flower girl, she saw him signal the DJ as he came back to where she sat.

The music started, slow and bluesy and he pulled her into his arms. She curled against him as he nuzzled her hair. If the world ended tomorrow, she thought, she would be content.

"I want to take you to the cottage, spread a blanket on the sand, and make love to you," he whispered in her ear. She felt his erection pressing into her middle, but heard reluctance in his voice.

"But?" she questioned.

"I have to leave," he said as he rubbed a hand down her back to her waist.

She tilted back to see his face. So much for contentment. She thought for sure this would be the night…she had so hoped it would be the night.

He looked as forlorn as she felt. "Since it's the Sheriff's daughter's wedding, he can't leave. He asked me and a few others to help patrol down at the West Bay."

"For the rock concert?" Her question drew a reluctant smile.

"Well, you're up on the current doings."

"It's a small island." She threw his words back at him.

"You can stay. I'll catch a ride with one of the guys and you can take the Jeep back."

She shook her head. "I'm ready if you are." There would be no sense staying if he wasn't there.

They said good bye to the bride and groom and walked through the darkness to his Jeep. In minutes, they were back at the B&B and she reluctantly let him pull her up the steps.

He turned to face her. His kiss was gentle, which was probably for the best. If he had given her any choice, she would have dragged him upstairs to her room.

"I want you," he whispered raggedly. "More than you know."

She doubted he could want any more than she did.

"Do what you need to do. We have all the time in the world." The words tasted bitter on her tongue because she knew that time was running out.

* * *

Cheyenne didn't hear from Jake the next day, but figured he was catching up on his sleep after staying up half the night at the concert. She ran into Lindsay late in the afternoon while out for a walk and found that not only had he spent the night keeping others out of trouble, a large group of them, herself included, had descended on West Bay that morning on trash patrol.

"You should have called me," Cheyenne said. "I can pick up litter."

"You wouldn't have wanted to handle the mess those people left behind. Honestly, what would it have hurt to throw a bottle into the trash can instead of at it? And that wasn't the worst of it." Lindsay shuttered.

"Then of course, there were the leftovers," Lindsay continued. "Even though the ferry extended its service until two in the morning, a large group couldn't see their way back to town, so just curled up on the beach and in the park. Jake helped the deputies round up the strays and point them towards the ferry port. From the smell of most of them, beer wasn't the only thing they inhaled last night."

Jake had no business being out in a crowd like Lindsay described. "When did you see him last?" She didn't want to call if he was sleeping, but she was worried.

"Oh, don't worry about Jake." Lindsay read her thoughts. "He dropped me off at my place around noon and said he was going home to sleep."

A twinge of jealousy appeared out of nowhere, causing her to purse her lips. She had no right to feel that way, but that didn't stop the feeling.

Lindsay took a phone call, then swung a leg over her bike. "Gotta go. You're one lucky lady, Cheyenne," she said with a sigh.

Cheyenne raised her brows in surprise.

"Not only is your man the handsomest devil I've seen in a long time, he has the hots for you. He couldn't quit talking about you while we were picking up trash."

Cheyenne laughed. "He's not *my man*, and I'm not sure that is a ringing endorsement."

Lindsay gave her a scowl. "Jake hasn't been on the island long, but he's made himself part of the community and everyone who is a lifetime resident adores him." She stopped then grinned. "Well, George Franklin and Cam Bristol probably don't *adore* him, but they like him well enough. When you first arrived, I would never have pegged you as his type, but you've changed and I think you're good for him. If that's a problem for you, then you should cut him loose because nobody wants to see him get hurt." She pedaled off without a backward glance, leaving Cheyenne to think about what she had said.

Sure, they had shared a few kisses; even some rather spectacular petting, but there was just too much difference between them. She was technically employed by him, for goodness sakes. And nothing that they had shared absolved her from her responsibility to the senior Mr. Donovan. There were only sixteen days left to convince Jake to return to Chicago. She thought about his parting remarks last night; about wanting to make love to her.

No, she adamantly told herself. She would not use her body to get him to comply with his uncle's wishes. There had to be another way.

* * *

Her phone pinged the next morning.
Jake: Have dinner with me tonight.
Her: Come back to Chicago with me.
Jake: It wasn't meant to be a negotiation. ☹
Her: I had to try. ;)
Jake: Please have dinner with me?
Her: Can we go somewhere that has silverware?
Jake: ☺ See you at eight.

Cheyenne went downstairs for breakfast. As she was enjoying her second cup of coffee, Mrs. Godfrey came and sat across from her.

"As always, you serve an incredible breakfast," Cheyenne said. The French toast today had been like nothing she had ever tasted; thick slices of bread with a batter that was sweet enough not to even need syrup and grilled to a crispy brown.

"It's a favorite, that's for sure," the older woman said. "Most of the guests will be leaving today since the festival is over, so I like to send them off with a hearty meal. Did you see the fireworks last night?"

Cheyenne frowned. In her concern for Jake, she had completely forgotten about the festival and all it entailed. And as busy as Jake had been, it must have slipped his mind also.

"No, but it's not like I haven't seen them before."

Mrs. Godfrey cocked her head. "You were in early last night. Why didn't that young man of yours take you down to the pier? Did you have a spat?"

Ah, village life, Cheyenne thought.

"He was helping the deputies down at West Bay."

Mrs. Godfrey nodded her head, as though that explained everything. "Jake Smith's a very nice man, and

109

helps out ever since the day he set foot on the island." She narrowed her gaze. "I hope nothing's amiss."

Cheyenne ground her teeth. Lord help her if the residents of Lockabee found out the real reason she was here. They'd probably push her off the ferry dock and make her swim to the mainland. She worked hard to force a smile.

"Everything's fine. In fact, he's asked me to dinner tonight, so I was wondering if my cleaning has come back."

Mrs. Godfrey beamed. "It arrived on the morning ferry and I hung it in the hall closet." Then she frowned. "Those suits don't seem quite the thing for here on the island. Do you have something a little more..." she paused and pursed her lips in thought.

Cheyenne hung her head in defeat. Not only were the residents fiercely protective of Jake but now they were offering fashion advice for dating him?

"I bought a dress, but I've already worn it several times. I suppose I could go back to the boutique."

Mrs. Godfrey looked at the wall clock. "Well, if Charlotte doesn't have anything fancy enough, you have time to catch the eleven o'clock ferry and take a look at the waterfront shops in Red Haven." She quickly put her hand over Cheyenne's. "I'm not saying Charlotte won't have what you want, but just in case she doesn't have your size...or something." The sentence dragged off and Cheyenne was sure Mrs. Godfrey now wondered if she would say something disparaging to the store owner.

"I'm sure I can find something. In fact, I'll go have a look right now." She stood, anxious to get away. It wasn't that all the islanders hadn't been gracious, which of course was probably normal since their livelihoods depended on tourist traffic. It was more that she wasn't used to the scrutiny she had received since coming here. Everyone knew everything. While she had told herself upon graduating community college that she would never be average again, she thought maybe now would be a good time to be part of an anonymous audience rather than the lead actress in a play where she didn't know the lines, much less exactly what was going to happen in the next act.

"Hello," the saleslady said when Cheyenne entered the boutique. "You're Lindsay's friend." The woman put out her hand. "I'm Charlotte. I hope you're enjoying your stay on the island."

"Thank you, I am very much. I hadn't intended to stay as long as I have, so I'm in need of more clothes." She absently flipped through some clothes on a rack, wondering why she had told the woman that.

She chuckled. "Sometimes unexpected delays can turn into unexpected surprises."

So true, she thought.

"What do you have for dresses?"

"Hmm. Casual or elegant?" Charlotte led her toward the back of the shop.

"You have elegant?" Cheyenne asked without thought, so quickly added, "I'm sorry. It's just that everything on the island appears to be quite casual."

Charlotte laughed. "You're right, of course. However, the Prince Hotel is more upscale than the smaller inns and B&B's, and their dining is quite exclusive, so we try to keep a few basics on hand in case someone comes unprepared. Is this a date with Jake?"

Cheyenne groaned. She should have known. "It's dinner, but I don't know where we're going and I'm not sure I'd call it a date." *Deflect gossip*; another rule of being a good executive assistant.

The woman, who appeared to be about her own age, smiled knowingly. "Honey, if I were going out with Jake Smith, I'd make sure it was a date." She pulled a dress from the rack. "This should work."

It was your basic little black dress. The slim creation hung from very thin straps that criss-crossed in both front and back. The straps and a band across the bottom of the bodice were made of sequins that shimmered as she held it up.

Cheyenne loved it, but wondered if it was too dressy and yet didn't know how to ask without offending the saleslady.

"You can't go wrong with black," Charlotte said. "Add this," she grabbed a red silk wrap from a nearby counter, "and it will be dashing with your coloring."

She was right. The dress slid over Cheyenne's hips to end just above her knees. The criss-cross straps accented her breasts, and the silk wrap gave it a splash of color. She came out of the dressing room to check herself in the full length mirror. Jake better not think she looked like a school teacher.

"You look divine," Charlotte said. "Now to accessorize." She talked her into a pair of silver loop earrings and bangle bracelets, then glancing at her hair, added a silver clip. "Wear your hair up," she said. "That will show off the line of your neck and the dress straps, which by the way are very sexy. Shoes?"

"I have heels that will work nicely," Cheyenne said, cringing already at the cost of a single outfit. As she turned to go back into the dressing room she glanced again in the mirror. This had better be worth it.

She spent the afternoon on correspondence. Regardless of the fact that she had permission to be here and not in the office, Mr. Donovan kept forwarding things for her to do. It made her feel a little less guilty for not having already told him about Jake. That was still a predicament for which she had no answer.

At five, she shut down her computer and soaked in a bubble bath. She repainted her toenails a bright red that matched the silk wrap. She powdered and primped and perfumed, and her stomach fluttered as badly as if she were going to her first prom. Which she had never done, but she was sure the feeling was similar.

At promptly eight, the room phone rang.

"Hello?"

It was Mrs. Godfrey. "Cheyenne, there's a lovely young man downstairs for you." She hung up with a giggle, and Cheyenne felt she was in a boarding house where no man was ever allowed past the front parlor. She gave one final glance in the mirror, grabbed her clutch (another purchase at the boutique as all she had was a handbag), and went downstairs.

His back was to her when she entered the parlor, and for a moment, she thought he was someone else. A navy blazer stretched the width of his shoulders and tapered down his lean hips. He wore beige dress pants, and she was suddenly very happy Charlotte had talked her into the dress. The only thing he hadn't changed was his hair, but she had grown fond of the beach boy look on him.

He sensed her presence and turned, his eyes lighting up as his gaze slid down her length and back up. He had finished his ensemble with a white dress shirt, open at the throat, which set off his deep tan. As his lips curved into a very seductive smile, he walked toward her.

"My, my. Don't you look fine, Cheyenne Tucker." He stopped in front of her and held out a single red rose. "A symbol of my esteem, yet meager in the light of your beauty."

She tried not to giggle, honestly she did, but the merry sound escaped her lips. "You did not just make that up."

He gave her a mocking look. "How can you doubt me?"

"Because nobody talks like that anymore, and especially no one has ever talked that way to me."

He took a step even closer and bent to her ear. "Then you have been hanging out with the wrong people because you are truly exquisite tonight."

She blushed. For as much as she had been around Jake lately, and even after the kisses they had shared, she was still a little uncertain about her appeal. She had never had a man look at her with the kind of adoration Jake did. It both elated and frightened her.

He kissed her cheek and stepped back, once again surveying her. He tilted his head to the side, gave a little *hmm*, and dug in his pocket, coming up with a small knife. "I think," he said as he flipped it open and cut the stem of the rose to no more than an inch, "this is needed right here." He then tucked the rose into her cleavage, his knuckles brushing gently against her skin. The sweet smell floated between them.

When she lifted her gaze to him, he was still staring at her breasts and the flower nestled between them.

"Do we have to go to dinner?" he whispered raggedly, his breath warm on her skin.

"But you dressed in a coat." Her answer was breathless.

"And you bought a new dress." His gaze darkened.

"You promised me silverware."

Her comment broke the moment and he laughed, kissing her on the nose. "Until later."

Chapter 11

Cheyenne wondered where Jake was taking her as he drove west down Main Street, then turned south to drive along the coast. The sun was low in the horizon and the blue water of the Pacific cast diamonds into the air as waves broke against the rocks.

"Have you been this way?" he asked.

"No. It's beautiful. A little fiercer than the protected harbor and ferry port."

He slowed so she could appreciate the view. "Except for Sunset Beach, this entire side of the island is cliffs."

"Then where are we going?" She turned toward him.

He glanced briefly at her before returning his gaze to the road, which curved inward then toward the edge of the cliff. He wasn't going fast and she wasn't afraid; more like in awe of the sheer drop-off with only a guardrail to protect them from mishap.

"Windy Harbor is down on the south end; a natural port protected from the pacific winds so a perfect place for a marina. It is also the home of the Lockabee Yacht Club. Very exclusive." He turned again to wiggle his brows.

"And your little motor boat qualifies you for membership?"

He laughed as he pulled into a parking spot. "No membership; just connections."

"Of course. I keep forgetting how adored you are by all the residents."

He shot her another quick glance as he got out of the Jeep and came around to her side. "You're kidding. Says who?"

"Everyone," she said exasperated. "Except apparently the sheriff and the bartender. They simply *like*; not *adore*."

She put her hand in his as he helped her out and closed the door behind her. He had a thoughtful expression as he led her into the Yacht Club but didn't say anymore as the Maitre D led them to a table by the window. Once they were seated and he had ordered a bottle of wine, he finally smiled.

"You say people like me?"

"Of course. You're famous and you play the piano like a dream."

"No, I don't care about that. I mean people *here* like me?"

Cheyenne was at a loss. "You don't care about the millions of adoring fans?"

Their wine arrived and he took a sip, nodded to the waiter who then poured them each a glass. Once he had set the bottle on the table and left, Jake raised his glass to hers.

"Here's to Jake Smith." A boyish grin crossed his face.

At her continued look of befuddlement, he explained. "Remember the day at the dock when you asked me why I wouldn't return to Chicago and I, in turn, asked you what you felt?"

She nodded. "And I said *sand*. I didn't understand at the time. I'm not sure I understand now."

"I have always wanted to belong; here I do, simply because I'm me. You don't know what it's like. I have friends who shake my hand without wanting an autograph. I can see the sunrise from the beach and not from the inside of a limo. I hear seagulls screech instead of applause."

"But you must enjoy playing. You were at the bar piano the other night."

"My whole life, from the time I was six years old, has revolved around music and performing."

"Because you have a gift."

He nodded. "But a gift that should be mine to give as I please. And you are right; I do enjoy music and playing, but that is quite different from performing."

The waiter returned to take their order.

"I haven't even looked at the menu," Cheyenne said.

"I'll order, if you'd like," Jake said.

While he discussed menu choices, she glanced around, noting several couples at other tables enjoying conversations that probably weren't as weighty as hers and Jake's. She found it odd that two men, though dressed casually in polo shirts and slacks, appeared to be in a very serious discussion. It didn't seem the place to hold a business meeting. They looked vaguely familiar but she couldn't place them. When they noticed her glancing their way, they quickly quit talking and stared in the opposite direction.

She turned her attention back to Jake, watching him as she sipped her wine, mulling over what he had said. He handed the menus back to the waiter and returned his gaze to her, his brown eyes intent. She suddenly understood. His life had been completely organized and promoted with concert and recording demands that must have finally pushed him beyond his limits. He was constantly on display and rarely had a moment to himself. The feel of sand beneath his feet was something ordinary; taken for granted by many but denied to the famous Joseph Donovan.

Their meal was brought out and while Jake attacked his with relish, her stomach rolled and she wondered if she would be able to eat a bite. Everything Jake said made sense, and that only made her predicament worse. How was she supposed to convince him to return to Chicago when she was no longer sure that was where he belonged?

Jake watched Cheyenne nit-pick at her food, barely eating. It wasn't hard to understand what she was thinking. Over the course of her time here, he had been trying to convince her of his choice to remain just as adamantly as she was trying to convince him to return to Chicago. The only question was which of them was making progress. At times, he felt somewhat guilty toward his uncle, but then someone like George Franklin would ask his help and Jake felt a sense of usefulness that had been lacking in his life.

With a sigh, Cheyenne began eating. She had apparently come to a decision but Jake wasn't about to ask her. He had no desire to find out that she was still set on her original course of action.

"The salmon was absolutely delicious," she finally said as she set her napkin beside her plate. "And nothing was fried," she teased.

"Come on; you have to admit you like it."

"My hips don't." She gave a mock frown.

"I like your hips," he said softly just to watch her blush. He raised his hand for the waiter and quickly took care of the bill. "Come on; let's get out of here." He took her hand and hurried out of the restaurant.

They were almost back to town when Jake looked in the rear view mirror with a frown. The same car had been following them since leaving the Yacht Club, which wouldn't be unusual as there was only one road back to Princetown from the south end of the island. But when he sped up or slowed down, so had the other car. Now, he quickly turned at the next corner onto a residential street, watching as the other car turned, too.

"Hold on," he said just before swerving in front of an oncoming car to turn left.

"What?" Cheyenne squealed.

"Does my dear uncle have anybody else on my tail?" he asked, not looking at her as he wove in and out of bicycle and rickshaw traffic. He cranked the wheel sharply to the right onto another side street.

"No," she managed to croak out.

He quickly glanced her way but couldn't tell from her expression if she was lying or scared.

"Are you sure?" He didn't give her time to answer before he turned again, driving into the local car wash, honking his horn.

"Hank, let us in," he shouted at the man lounging lazily in a plastic lawn chair. "Hurry!"

Hank moved with surprising speed for a man of his age, pushing the button for the overhead door.

"You ain't got your top up." He pointed to the open jeep.

"Don't start the washer; just bring the door down fast." Jake drove into the wash bay and glanced behind him, holding his breath as the door came slowly down.

"Oh my God. What is going on?" Cheyenne turned to him.

He frowned. "You tell me. Nobody's bothered me until you showed up."

She was shaking her head before he had finished. "No. When Mr. Donovan asked me to find you, I suggested he use a professional investigation service but he refused. He said it would cause unwanted publicity."

Jake snorted. "Of course. Uncle is all about appearances. Still," he hesitated. He had once accused her of trying to seduce him for his uncle's purposes. Had he been so wrong about her?

Cheyenne pulled her cell out of her purse. "I'll prove it." Even though it was late, she punched in a number and then put it on speaker. When his uncle answered, Jake drew back. It wasn't the arrogant, domineering voice he was used to; but rather was weak and shallow.

"Mr. Donovan, it's Cheyenne Tucker."

"Have you found him?" The question was followed by a cough and wheeze.

Jake started to grab her phone but she batted his hand away. She looked him directly in the eyes, then said, "No, Mr. Donovan, I haven't found Joseph."

Jake relaxed.

"Then why are you wasting my time?" Now the voice sounded more like the man Jake knew.

"Because there seem to be some men following uh…me."

"You must be close. If there were any leaks as to where you went, there are always paparazzi trying to sniff out a story."

"I didn't tell anyone I was leaving town."

"Not even that little sister of yours?" She frowned at his uncle's question.

"Don't call until you have news." There was a definite click as his uncle hung up.

"I," Cheyenne started as a loud knocking on his door diverted Jake's attention.

"Somebody looking fer you?" Hank asked, then turned to the side to spit a stream of tobacco on the cement.

"Did you see anyone suspicious?" Jake countered.

"Might of."

Jake dug in the console and handed the old man some bills.

"Max Brannigan's old Corsica cruised by."

"Why would you think Max was suspicious?"

"Cuz it was Max's car but it weren't Max driving." Another stream hit the ground.

"Are you sure?"

The old man's bushy eyebrows scrunched. "Eyesight's as good now as at twenty." He then looked past Jake to Cheyenne. "And I always 'preciate a looker." He winked at her before swinging his gaze back to Jake. "'Sides, Max's too old to be driving anymore, so he sits at the ferry port and rents out his car to tourists who're too lazy to walk."

"Thanks, Hank. You're a pal." Jake reached over and laid his hand on the man's arm.

"Yeah, well, if'n that was true, you'd get that darned boat fixed and take me fishing."

Jake laughed. "It's done. I just haven't had time to go fishing."

Hank tilted his head, giving Cheyenne another wink. "I can see why. You might take your young lady out on a moonlight cruise."

"She's not—"

"I'm not—" Cheyenne said at the same time.

Hank laughed as he walked away. Another minute passed before the front door of the bay slowly rose.

Jake cleared his throat before turning to Cheyenne. "I think that car followed us from the Marina, which means whoever it is apparently recognized us at the restaurant."

"There were two men at the restaurant who kept looking at us," she said. "I'm sure I've seen them somewhere before."

"They may have been the same ones who took pictures at the bar the other night. Even if they were mistaken about my identity then, I need to find out who they are. Until I do, we probably shouldn't go back to my place, and I doubt the Inn is any safer for you."

Cheyenne was staring straight ahead but Jake saw her hands shaking in her lap. He reached over and covered them with his. "It's all right. I'll keep you safe. I have a friend; we can go to his place."

"That's not it." She shook her head, finally looking at him. "I lied, Jake, to my employer. I don't lie."

"Never?" He tried to tease a smile from her but she fiercely shook her head.

"I doubt you'll go to hell for what you said." He cautiously exited the car wash and turned onto the street. "Look at it this way. It wasn't actually a lie. You didn't find Joseph; he doesn't really exist."

He called Trevor to make sure he was home and then took the next turn and they were quickly out of town. The dirt road led into Diamond National Park which covered almost half of the eastern side of the island. His friend was a forest ranger and had a cabin deep in the woods. With modern surveillance technology throughout the woods to detour troublemakers, along with the traditional ranger's tower, they would know if anyone was coming for miles around.

As he wound along the dirt road which was little more than a path, he also called George.

"Why would anyone driving Max's old car be following you?" the sheriff asked when Jake explained his situation.

"I have no idea. You might keep an eye out for them and find out."

Trevor was waiting on the porch when they pulled up. "You didn't have to dress up just to come visiting," he grinned as he shook Jake's hand. When Jake saw his eyes

121

light up as he turned toward Cheyenne, he squeezed the ranger's hand a little tighter. The man looked at him, brows raised.

"This is Cheyenne; a *close* friend." Jake emphasized the word, which only made Trevor's grin broader.

"Oh, no," Cheyenne wailed and quickly moved past Trevor, ignoring his outstretched hand to quickly climb the steps onto the porch. It was then Jake noticed the yipping coming from a box in the far corner.

"Are you allergic to dogs?" Trevor asked.

Cheyenne didn't even answer as she walked right to the box and squatted down, her short black dress rucking up her thighs to show even more of her bare leg. Jake watched Trevor's eyes widened and he smacked him on the arm.

"Aren't you precious?" Cheyenne cooed as she lifted one wiggly mass, holding it up to rub her cheek against its soft fur.

"Apparently not," Trevor answered his own question, shooting a questioning glance at Jake.

Jake continued to watch Cheyenne. The stern and rigid Miss Tucker was a mass of emotions as she stood, puppy in hand and gazed at him with watery eyes. She cuddled the puppy to her breasts and took a seat on the nearby swing. Damned if he wasn't jealous of a dog.

He kept his gaze on her as he told his friend, "We need a place to hang out for a few days."

"Does it have anything to do with the sheriff looking for Max's car?" Trevor's question had Jake swiveling his gaze.

"How do you know that?"

Trevor laughed. "This is Lockabee Island, friend." And that explained everything. "Besides, I have a police scanner in the tower, where I happened to be until I saw you drive up."

Cheyenne laughed and the sound floated across his shoulders like a caress. He thought briefly about the musical score he had composed based on that sound for it was rich and full; not a feminine giggle or trill. He turned to watch her. Regardless of the fancy dress and heels she wore, she now had two puppies in her lap and a third cuddled under her chin.

"You are adorable." She kissed one on the head before looking up and catching him watching her. Her smile faltered for an instant but then the puppy licked her chin and her eyes regained their sparkle.

Jake's stomach dropped to his toes. She was the one who was adorable, he thought. If he hadn't been aware of it before, he now realized he was in so much trouble.

* * *

Cheyenne reluctantly put the puppies back in their box when Trevor said he took them in the house at night so wild animals wouldn't get them. He closed the door, leaving her and Jake alone on the porch.

She moved to where he leaned against the porch rail, arms crossed, gaze intent on her.

"You seem to have made plenty of friends in a short time," she said by way of conversation. She suddenly realized how quiet it was and how alone they were, even with his friend in the cabin. Her heart sped up.

"It's easy, if you open yourself to it," he replied.

"I feel like we've become friends," she said.

Her comment caused him to spin toward her, bracing his hands on the rail, effectively pinning her in place.

"I don't want to be your friend," he stated emphatically. His mouth was drawn down in a frown and his dark eyes snapped. She looked at him in alarm.

"No, Cheyenne." His voice was dangerously soft as he leaned closer. "I want much, much more."

Always before, his kisses had started out gentle, but not tonight. He ravaged her mouth, forcing her lips apart to delve in with his tongue, setting her on fire. She longed for him to touch her, but his hands remained firmly on the railing. She settled for the next best thing by circling his neck with her arms, tugging him close until their chests touched.

"God, I want you." He tore his mouth from hers long enough to whisper. Hot nips of his lips coursed down her neck and across the top of her bodice to linger near where the rose was still tucked. His tongue licked across her skin, making her whimper. She sank her fingers in his hair to hold him in place.

She wanted to beg him; to finally have him quench the flames he kept igniting throughout her entire body. She didn't care what tomorrow brought; didn't care if he went back to Chicago or stayed here in anonymity the rest of his life. All she cared about was easing the deep ache he created with a single touch.

The sound of a crash and swearing broke them apart, although Jake didn't move far. He finally lifted a hand to her cheek, rubbing her lips with his thumb. A faint smile touched his lips. "It's seems we are destined once again for an intermission between movements." He kissed where his thumb had lingered. "But you have my word; this symphony is going to reach a climax as soon as humanly possible."

* * *

Jake could have easily trounced Trevor for interrupting his time with Cheyenne. He made sure his friend knew his displeasure when he escorted Cheyenne into the small cabin. The more he frowned, the more Trevor grinned. As he explained the sleeping arrangements, Jake decided his friend was probably right. When he made love to Cheyenne, he wanted it to be at a time and place where no one and nothing could interrupt. The way he felt at this moment, that was going to mean at least a day; possibly several; alone with her.

"There's only one bedroom, so I put on clean sheets for Cheyenne," Trevor stated. "The bathroom is the door on the right."

"Oh, I don't want to take your bed," she replied shyly.

"It's okay. Jake and I will bunk on sleeping bags out here." He looked over at the couch, where two Black Labs, apparently the parents of the litter, had taken up residence. "Unless Jake wants to wrestle Romeo and Juliet for a spot on a lumpy couch."

Jake looked from the dogs to where Cheyenne was closing the door to the bathroom. As he stripped down to his briefs, he wondered for a moment how long it would take Trevor to go to sleep and if the dogs would be quiet enough for him to sneak into Cheyenne's bed. In the end, he barely heard the doors open and close as everyone settled down for the night.

* * *

Jake opened blurry eyes as the sound of voices filtered into his head. When he heard Cheyenne's soft laugh, he came more fully awake. Damning Trevor for crowding his space, he quickly sat up only to find Trevor in the kitchen and Cheyenne sitting on the floor near him with the puppies already on her lap. At his sudden movement, one puppy turned, then bounded in his direction, trying to claw his way up Jake's bare chest.

"Ouch, damn." He lifted the puppy away only to have yet another try the same trick. Cheyenne quickly reached over and snagged the second pup, her fingers briefly contacting his chest. Sparks immediately flew as he sucked in a breath and caught her gaze. Her eyes were huge, her cheeks dusted with color and when he glanced down, her chest rose and fell with rapid breathing. It was all he could do not to groan. As it was, he bunched the sleeping bag around his hips to hide the evidence of his desire.

Trevor cleared his throat. "There's coffee and biscuits for breakfast but that's about all.

It's grocery run today or we'll be eating *guessing stew* for dinner."

Cheyenne got up from the floor, graceful even in her short dress and walked over to the kitchen area. It was just the opportunity Jake needed to hurry to the bedroom with his clothes. He returned just as Cheyenne asked what Trevor meant.

125

"It's anybody's guess what's in it." He laughed, but Cheyenne looked ill.

"Are there usually…wild animals in it?"

"Nothing's in season or there probably would be." The ranger grabbed his hat from a peg by the door. "If you put the pups in the box on the porch, they should be fine for the time I'll be gone. I don't go often so usually spend most of the day in town when I do."

Jake swung his gaze to his friend, wondering at the message behind his words. When he winked, Jake understood perfectly.

The minute the door closed, he hurried into the bathroom, borrowed his friend's razor, and used his finger to rub toothpaste across his teeth. It would have to do. He came out to find her nowhere in the house. When he went out on the porch, the puppies were in their box, the larger dogs lying quietly in the shade. His gaze moved out across the small yard where he found her, barefoot, wiggling her toes in the grass and looking toward the tower. Inspiration struck.

"Would you like to see the island from up there?" he asked coming up behind her. Even in the same clothes she had worn the night before, she smelled of sunshine and sweetness but he didn't dare touch her. If he did, he would take her right there in the yard. He wanted her that badly.

She turned to smile at him; her eyes alight with avid curiosity. "Could we?" she asked and Jake's knees threatened to give out. He only hoped he could make it up the ladder to the tower. That task became an almost insurmountable feat as he let her go ahead of him to insure her safety. Her long legs stretched from rung to rung, calf muscles bunching but it was her fanny, barely covered by her dress from his vantage point, that had him sucking for oxygen when they reached the top.

"Oh, my, what a spectacular view," she said, slowly walking the perimeter of the small room, her gaze soaking it all in.

Spectacular was right, thought Jake as he watched her draw a deep breath, her breasts threatening to overflow the bodice of her dress.

"How can one island have everything – lakes, mountains, forest?"

He managed to pull his gaze away from her. "You've never seen any of that before?" Off to one side was a crystal blue lake, the water sparkling in the sun. He could see Mount Lockabee to the south. Everything else within view was forest, the thick canopy of trees concealing the streams that were part of the landscape and the spots where campgrounds stood.

She shrugged carelessly. "I grew up in west Texas; pretty flat and dry."

"Ah, the elusive Miss Tucker leaks a fact."

She narrowed her gaze. "It was no secret. I had to put everything on my job application."

"Which I have never seen." He definitely didn't want to talk about her job. He slowly came toward her. "I find it interesting how little I really know about you, and yet how much I want you."

He watched reluctance flair ever so briefly across her features but he was not to be denied. He knew what would happen when they came together. He stepped close, raising a finger to trace the criss-cross straps of her dress, ending at the very center point where her breasts pushed up. He replaced his finger with his lips, but the instant he tasted her, fire consumed him.

He fumbled finding the hidden zipper to her dress. She tugged his shirt out of his trousers and when she couldn't immediately get it unbuttoned, he jerked it over his head. She stood before him in bra and panties and his hands shook as he reached for her.

"You are gorgeous." His palms slid across her shoulders and down her arms. She smiled almost shyly. "Tell me you want this."

At his comment, her gaze flew to his. "Why would you even ask that?"

He gave a shrug. "Insecurities?"

She gave a small laugh. "The great Joseph Donovan has performance insecurities?"

He shook his head. "It's Jake, and I want you so badly, I'm afraid I'll hurt you in my frenzy."

"You could never hurt me," she replied as she reached for his belt, then unbuttoned his trousers.

He found a sleeping bag in the corner and spread it out on the floor. She came to him without hesitation and he lay down beside her, pulling her close. There was no more talk, the only sounds were her sighs as he kissed her from head to toe and back, lingering at her stomach to lick her belly button before making his way up to her breasts. She was full and lush and his hands caressed her reverently.

She did not lie quietly beneath him, but continuously ran her hands up and down his back, delving beneath his trousers to squeeze his butt. He managed to tug his pants down and kicked them across the room before settling between her thighs.

"Now," she gasped as he rubbed against her mound.

"I want this to last."

She shook her head, urging him on with hands on his butt as she slid her feet up his thighs and planted them on the pad beneath them. "Kiss me, Jake."

He almost smiled at her demands but he was just as impatient. He took her mouth, and she grabbed his head, slanting her lips across his. He lifted his hips and unerringly found her center, sliding deep inside. Her legs came up to wrap around him and fireworks started.

Cheyenne practically came unglued the moment Jake entered her. Her muscles clutched and though she wanted to relax and take him deeper, her body refused to obey. And then he began to move and she opened to him. All her senses came alive from her breath taking in the scent of him to the feel of him moving against and in her. She welcomed the weight of his body pressing her down.

The rhythm changed; quickened as he braced on his elbows and gazed down at her. His hips came to hers again and again and she felt the tremors begin. Before she could gasp a breath, her body tensed and released, sensations

128

shooting through her from the center of her to the very tips of her fingers and toes.

She tipped her head back to find him watching her. His hips slowed to a stop, his gaze never leaving hers.

"I am beyond words; watching you; feeling you."

"Then show me." She caressed his cheek as he bent to kiss her; her heels digging into his back to urge him on.

Almost frantic, Jake lifted her hips to thrust deeper, pumping fast, then slow, pushing her up the peak again. When her gaze widened and her mouth opened, he dropped his head, lightly biting the tender flesh between her shoulder and neck and she bucked beneath him, crying out his name as she came. Her release triggered his and he throbbed within her for endless moments. Even when he could catch his breath, he continued peppering kisses along her chest and breasts. He couldn't get enough of her, and the thought amazed him.

"Stop," she giggled as he licked the bud of her breast.

He ignored her and sucked it into his mouth, molding the shape of her with his hand.

She pushed against his shoulders. "Stop, please. It's too sensitive."

He raised his head to meet her gaze.

"I'm sensitive," she corrected. "Every nerve in my body is screaming."

He grinned, enjoying the fact that he had turned the reticent Miss Tucker into a quivering mass of nerves. With a sigh, he rolled to his back beside her, utterly replete.

"You sound very pleased with yourself," she said.

He could only manage to turn his head, but when he found her smiling at him, he wondered how long it would take before he could make love to her again.

"I think the feeling is mutual," he replied, only to watch her eyes shutter, blocking him from sensing her thoughts.

Cheyenne definitely concurred with the pleasure they had shared but now she felt a sense of disquiet. Time was running out. As she felt Jake relax beside her, she thought perhaps he might be open to persuasion.

"What's the date?" she asked cautiously, although she well knew there were only fourteen days to her deadline.

Jake lifted his arm to look at his watch, a rather plain Timex on a leather band instead of the Rolex he had always worn.

"The fifteenth," he answered then she heard a change in tone as he added, "Why?"

She turned to him, propping her chin on his chest. She breathed him in, the scent of their lovemaking lingering on his skin. "Would you please consider returning to Chicago?"

The moment she uttered the words, she knew it was a mistake. He stiffened beneath her, his eyes darkening. She watched his jaw clench before he roughly pushed her aside and got to his feet.

He jammed his legs into his trousers, his movements jerky, his back taut with anger. She needed to explain.

"Jake? I—"

"Shut up! Just shut the hell up!" He rounded on her and she leaned back, frightened by the fierceness of his expression. "I should have known," he muttered as though to himself, running his fingers through his hair.

Cheyenne tucked her knees under her chin and wrapped her arms around her legs, suddenly aware of her nakedness. She didn't say a word, hoping he wouldn't come to the wrong conclusion before she could explain.

Her hopes were dashed with his next words.

"I can't believe my uncle would use you," he paused, then rephrased. "No, that's not true; he would. I guess what I can't believe is that *you* would use your body to lure me into his trap."

She gasped at his cruel words.

He then gave her such a look of disgust she cringed. He turned from her as though he couldn't bare the sight of her.

She scrambled to her feet, picking up his discarded shirt and pulling it on. "Jake, please. It's not what you think."

"Shit." He had been looking out the opening but now turned back. "Where's my phone?" He jerked the sleeping bag up; dug through his pockets and scanned the floor. "Where the hell is my phone?"

She didn't understand the swift need to call anyone, especially when she was trying to make amends, but offered the only suggestion she could think of. "Maybe in the coat you left in the cabin?"

He headed for the entryway but when she tried to follow he put up his hand. "Stay away from me." His eyes still blazed with anger. "In fact, get the hell out of my life."

She crumbled to the floor, tears obscuring her last view of him as he disappeared down the trap door.

In minutes she heard the roar of a motor and dragged herself up to the window opening in time to see Jake fly by on a four wheeler. It would appear he couldn't get away from her fast enough. As she watched him disappear into the trees, smoke came into view and she raised her gaze to see a tell-tale stream of gray lifting into the sky.

That's what Jake had seen, she thought, but suddenly gasped, her gaze dropping to the point she had last seen him, then up again to the line of smoke. Jake was driving straight toward a fire.

She curled into a ball, sobbing. What had she done?

Chapter 12

It was hours before Cheyenne heard the sound of an approaching vehicle. In that time she had gone from remorse to anger and back to remorse. Jake's words had hurt her terribly and she kept telling herself he didn't mean them. Then anger surfaced and she blamed him for not listening to her, but then depression finally set in. She knew from the look on Jake's face as he left that he would not believe anything she had to say. She curled tightly into a ball on the couch, pulling his shirt closer around her. She inhaled the scent lingering in the fabric and cried.

The truth was she felt compassion for both Mr. Donovan and Jake; two stubborn men who refused to back down. Jake wanted control over his own life, and Mr. Donovan was trying desperately to find the fame through Jake that had eluded him all his life.

Somewhere in the approaching darkness, she realized it wasn't about her job anymore, or the responsibility she felt toward her employer. She wanted the two to reconcile because she had never had the opportunity to do that with her own mother. She knew if something happened to the elder Donovan, it would eat at Jake forever.

When the vehicle stopped outside, she rose and opened the door. A bare-chested Trevor was on the porch with a similarly clad Jake slumped against his side.

"Oh, dear lord, what happened?" She raced to Jake's other side to grab his arm in support only to find his hand wrapped in what appeared to be a blood soaked shirt.

"Long story," Trevor replied, shuffling Jake to a chair at the small table by the kitchen. "Grab some towels and the first aid kit from the bathroom."

"We've got to get him to a doctor," she cried, barely able to think. Why did it have to be his hand?

"I called but Doc's on the mainland until tomorrow. Besides it was closer to bring him back here. Get the kit," he reiterated as he began running water in a basin at the sink.

She turned to go but Jake grabbed her wrist. His eyes were unfocused and his speech slurred, but he still managed to growl, "What are you doing here? I told you to go away."

She heard Trevor swear but couldn't force herself to look at him as she hurried away.

She returned to hear Trevor say, "This is going to hurt," just as he plunged Jake's hand into the basin of water. Jake jerked and batted at his friend with his free hand, but Trevor held on. Cheyenne dropped the towels and kit on the table and hurried around to grab Jake's arm.

"He's trying to help," she said softly. Jake struggled another minute before slumping forward in the chair.

"Did he faint?" she whispered.

Trevor gave her a slight smile. "Guys don't faint. We pass out, which he may have done but that's not good. He got hit on the back of the head so he may have a concussion." He turned to look at the basin, now dark pink with blood. "I'll worry about that after I see to this cut."

He lifted Jake's hand out of the water and placed it palm up on a towel. A long gash sliced across the heel of his hand, blood still seeping from the wound. He spread the ragged edges and Jake groaned but didn't stir.

"It's not as deep as you'd think, given the amount of blood," he said. "Luckily there doesn't appear to be any muscle cut, but it's going to need stitched up." He looked over at her. "How strong is your stomach?"

Cheyenne's legs grew weak, but when she looked at Jake's face, bruised and covered with soot, she knew she would do whatever it took to help. Even if he didn't want her help; even if he wanted her out of his life.

"You should know," she started.

Trevor interrupted. "The bump on his head caused him to mouth off."

She sadly shook her head, squeezing her eyes shut as tears threatened. He lifted her chin but didn't say anything until she looked at him.

"It can be fixed; whatever it is, but first we have to fix him."

She took a deep breath and nodded. "What do you need me to do?"

"This is going to sound bizarre but it's the only way I can think of to get it done. Unconscious or not he's going to fight me when I start on his hand. If I leave him in the chair, he'll end up on the floor anyway, so he might as well start there. Besides, it will give us leverage." Carefully, he lowered Jake to the floor, stretching his left arm out on the towel.

He returned to the table and opened the first aid kit, taking out a bottle of alcohol, salve, several bandages and finally a threaded needle, which he held out to her.

"God, no. I can't sew him up." She bit her lip to stop the trembling.

"It's okay. I'll do the honors, but I need you to sterilize it with the alcohol as I pour it over his hand."

"That's going to hurt, isn't it?" *Stupid question,* she scolded.

"Oh, yeah, like demons from hell chewing on you. That's why I need you to sit on his legs to help hold him down. I'll have my knee on his arm, but it might not be enough."

It wasn't. The minute alcohol hit the gash, Jake bucked and jerked. Cheyenne braced her knees on either side of him and grabbed the table to keep from falling over but her weight was hardly enough to hold him down. She could see Trevor clench his teeth as Jake pounded on his back.

"Damnfuckingsonofabitch!!!" Jake railed. Cheyenne blushed and Trevor snorted.

"Wish I could drown your hurt in whiskey, buddy." The hurt in his voice echoed Cheyenne's thoughts.

"Get ready again. I want to make sure it's disinfected."

Whether it was due to the concussion or sheer pain, Jake didn't even twitch the second time Trevor doused his hand. She handed him the needle, her hand shaking.

"Don't watch," he cautioned and she turned her head to the side. "How about I take your mind off things by telling you what happened?"

"*That* will take my mind off things?"

He laughed. "Probably true." He was quiet but Cheyenne didn't dare look at what he was doing.

"Do you think there will be any lasting damage?" she braved the question.

"If you're asking whether he'll still be able to play the piano, I'd say probably, though we'll get him into Doc's first thing tomorrow."

She didn't hear anything past the first part of his comment. She swiveled to see him.

His gaze remained intent on his work. "Yes, I know who he really is; he told me. No, not everyone on the island knows but even if they did, they'd respect his privacy."

Cheyenne breathed a sigh of relief until his next words. "That was another reason I brought him here instead of into town. From what I know, someone's looking for you, or him, or both of you seeing as you're tangled together somehow."

"I work for his uncle."

"So he said." He frowned at his work. "Good thing this isn't his face. I'm not much for sewing other than patching a pair of jeans now and again and nobody sees that except for the deer."

Cheyenne stared at Trevor; a friend keeping a secret, a man willing to do whatever needed done for his friend. Jake was truly blessed to have found this place.

"Tell me what happened," she said when the silence lingered and all she could think of was a needle piercing skin.

"Jake called me about a fire and I asked him to bring the four wheeler, which has a large water barrel, and I'd meet him at the location. It would have taken useless time if I had to come back here then out again and all I had in the truck was a small extinguisher. Anyway, he got there before me and whoever had lost control of their campfire was trying to get away. Jake chased him down while I doused the fire, but he got hurt in the process."

His voice had risen in anger toward the end. "Damn campers anyway, building fires in restricted areas. We're lucky the whole forest didn't ignite."

"What happened to the firebug?" Only the two of them had returned in the truck.

Trevor slanted her a grin. "He's currently roped to a tree on site. I was more worried about Jake." He sat back and rolled his head, trying to loosen tight muscles. "Hand me that salve and bandages."

"Should we move him to the couch?" she asked as Trevor finally stood, putting out a hand to help her to her feet.

"He'll be alright there for another few minutes. We're going to have to wake him up anyway because of the concussion so we'll let him walk instead of me carrying him." He collected the ruined towels and disposed of the basin contents as she put things back in the first aid kit.

"You'd better put alcohol on your next shopping list," she said.

"Damn. I had groceries in the truck." He hurried out the door and came back carrying two canvas bags and another bag with a familiar logo.

He set the canvas bags on the counter and handed her the other one. "This is for you. Jake asked me to pick you up a few things in town. Apparently he figured you needed something other than that black dress." He grinned as his gaze traveled down her length. "I'd say he was right."

Until that moment, Cheyenne had forgotten she wore Jake's shirt, which only came to mid-thigh. She tugged at the hem, her face heating rapidly.

Trevor pretended not to notice her discomfiture as he began putting groceries away. "You might do me a favor, though, when you get back to town. While Charlotte knew your size and didn't mind picking out a few things, she kept asking me questions as to why I was the one buying you clothes. Even when I told her to charge them to Jake, the questions didn't end."

"Didn't you tell her what happened?"

"No sense in starting gossip. Besides, it wouldn't have made any difference but for one thing."

He turned as Jake groaned. They both crouched down beside him. Trevor tapped him lightly on the cheek. "Wake up, buddy. Come on, open those baby blues."

"They're brown," Cheyenne automatically corrected only to have him grin again.

"Of course you would know."

She scowled at him. "What one thing?"

"Huh? Oh, that. Charlotte and I are," he paused as if not sure what to say.

"In a relationship?" Cheyenne immediately understood.

"Right. And she tends to be a little sensitive." He tapped Jake's cheek again, eliciting a groan.

"I'll make sure she understands." Together, the two of them hefted Jake into a sitting position as he slowly opened his eyes.

His gaze found hers and his eyes narrowed. "Are you still mad at me?" he asked to her surprise.

"And well she should be," Trevor said before she could form a thought. "Don't worry about that now. We're going to move you to the couch and then you're going to drink some water and try to stay awake."

Cheyenne wasn't much help as Jake lumbered to his feet, supported by Trevor. She did manage to get a glass of water but questions raced through her mind. Why was Jake confused? Why did Trevor take her side when he most likely knew where the fault lay?

As she helped Jake down some of the water, Trevor explained. "A concussion can cause confusion and many times, the events just prior or after a blow to the head are forgotten, or skewed. You should try to keep him awake, but if he falls asleep, wake him up every two hours."

"Me? Where are you going?"

"I still have to take the firebug to town and do the paperwork to press charges," he said as he walked into the bedroom, leaving the door ajar so she could hear him. "I'm going to take Jake's Jeep instead of the truck." He came out wearing a fresh uniform. "If someone is still looking for you and they see the Jeep, it might help deflect interest when you're not in it."

That seemed a good idea. What wasn't such a great idea was leaving Jake in her care. "What if something happens here? What if he develops a fever?"

"Nothing is going to happen. Just keep an eye on him and get him to drink."

"But…" The door closed behind the ranger.

"Damn, my head hurts," Jake said and she hurried back around the couch to stand in front of him.

"There's aspirin in the first aid kit. Shall I get you some?"

"No! No drugs."

"Jake, it's only aspirin." She didn't understand his adamant refusal but he kept shaking his head, then his eyes drifted closed.

"No, no, stay awake." She shook him slightly until his eyes opened again.

"Talk to me; keep me awake."

At least he didn't sound mad at her, and for a moment she thought about curling on the couch beside him. When his gaze traveled down her bare legs and back up, she decided that wasn't a good idea. She dragged a chair over from the table and sat in front of him.

"What should we talk about?" She certainly wasn't going to bring up one topic in particular.

"Why don't you like me?" Jake asked. Even though his head and hand hurt like the devil, her voice was soothing and he really did want to know.

"I never said that," she replied too quickly.

"Let me rephrase. Why don't you like the image of me?" She seemed to like Jake Smith well enough. An image of a slinky black dress sliding down her curves flittered across his mind but he couldn't grasp it long enough to know if it were real or imaginary.

She looked away and he thought she wouldn't answer. He sat until the silence stretched into minutes. He reached over and touched a finger to her chin, turning her back to face him. A look of sorrow washed over her features before she schooled her expression.

"You have everything," she emphasized the last word. "Everything. Fame, fortune, family. And you threw it all away."

"I didn't throw it away." What should it matter to her anyway?

"Semantics. Walking away is the same thing."

Suddenly, concussion and throbbing headache aside, he understood. He had it all, or so she thought, and apparently she did not. Or at least she had not come from money as he had. He racked his brain for a change in topic.

"Cheyenne. That's a unique name. I thought you said you were from Texas."

Her expression cleared, her shoulders relaxed. "Although I don't remember him, Mom said our dad was from Wyoming. My name is probably no more unique than my sister's. She's named Laramie Katherine." She smiled softly. "I used to call her Lark."

"And what did she call you?"

She hesitated, but finally said, "Cat."

"Why?"

"Because of my middle name." She handed him a water glass and he emptied it. Without his asking, she got up and went to refill it. She came back and sat again in front of him and he cursed his aching body for he desperately wanted to touch her lovely legs.

Trying to get his mind out of the gutter, he went back to playing *Twenty Questions*. "Getting information out of you is worse than practicing my scales when I was ten.

BCDEFGABC, over and over again. How many times do I have to ask why?"

She laughed and he was happy to hear it. Laughter had been severely missing from his life. On the downside, her smile transformed her face from sweet to seductive. Again, an image flashed in his brain; something that had made him incredibly angry, and then it was gone. Yet he knew it had something to do with the woman sitting barefoot across from him in what looked suspiciously like his shirt.

"Are you going to tell me?"

She reached across and took his glass, sipping some water. "Cheyenne Alyce Tucker," she said. "Cat."

From the beginning, everything about this woman had fascinated him but now he knew he would never be able to think of her as Miss Tucker again. His eyes drifted closed. "See, that wasn't so hard."

* * *

Cheyenne let him sleep two hours, then woke him again. His headache was a little better, he said, but his hand throbbed and he finally consented to taking aspirin.

"Tell me more about Cheyenne Alyce Tucker," he prompted after dutifully drinking an entire glass of water. She had made coffee while he slept and she now sipped the hot brew.

"I'm not a very interesting person," she said.

"I know better," he argued. "Where did you go to school? Did you lose your virginity at prom?" He wiggled his brows.

"I'm not going to tell you that!"

He smiled and she thought again how handsome he was, although that wasn't what had drawn her to him. He was kind, thoughtful and helpful; friendly and generous. Making love to him had been the stuff of dreams. At the moment, he didn't remember his anger but she couldn't count on him never remembering what had caused him to tear off into the forest.

140

Perhaps it would be best to tell him the truth about herself. Then, when he remembered what he considered her betrayal, he would realize he was better off without her.

"I told you not so long ago that I never lie, but that *was* a lie." She held up a hand when he started to speak. "You need to know this, and I won't get through it if you keep interrupting."

At his nod, she continued. "Unlike your mother, mine was rather absent minded about Lark and me, sometimes leaving us for days at a time as she partied with her current boyfriend." She looked away when he frowned. It was far too late for sympathy. "We moved from town to town, whenever we got evicted for not making rent, until finally one day, our mom moved on without us."

"Geez. How old were you?"

"Luckily by that time I was sixteen; Lark was thirteen. I made the mistake of filing a missing person report and when the police came they were going to turn us over to social services. So I lied and told them I was eighteen and had legal guardianship of my sister. When I told him I didn't know where the papers were to prove that, he said he would come back the next day." She closed her eyes at the memory. "The next day, we were gone."

She sighed before continuing. She might as well tell him everything. "It was also a lie when I said I had never done anything wrong. I stole boxes of Macaroni and Cheese to feed us when I didn't have a job."

That brought a slight smile to his lips. "No wonder you made a face at my humble cooking."

She looked away, unable to meet his gaze but his words had her turning back.

"You did what you had to do, Cheyenne. There's nothing wrong with that."

"Don't you see? I'm nothing but a fraud. We moved to a small nowhere town and stayed in a rundown hotel, cleaning rooms for a roof over our heads. I worked two jobs and went to community college while Lark finished school and I promised myself I would never, *never,* be poor again. I would never have people look down at me for being 'just a waitress'."

She gave a bitter laugh. "With my first paycheck from Donovan Academy I paid my rent and spent the rest on clothes and shoes."

Jake heard the raw emotion in every word she spoke. It was as if a knife had been lodged in his chest and he longed to hold her tight. What courage it must have taken for her to take charge of her life. It suddenly became quite clear as to why she had always been so rigid and efficient. And that was where she was truly wrong.

"Do you know," he said softly, "I think Miss Tucker is the real fraud."

Her head snapped up at his words. He reached over and took her hand, rubbing his thumb over the soft skin of her palm. When she tried to pull back, he held on tighter.

"No matter the clothes, the tight bun, the attitude, you're not really the stern and brusque Miss Tucker. You're courageous, strong and caring; as adorable as those puppies and you look great in my shirt."

Predictably she blushed. He scooted forward on the couch and leaned in to kiss her; a gentle brush of the lips with the promise of tomorrow.

"I think I'm good now," he said, lying down with his head on a pillow. "You need to get some sleep."

"Are you sure?" she questioned.

"Go to bed."

She got up and turned toward the bedroom but when he said her name, *Cat,* she turned back.

"Thank you for trusting me with your story." The rest of what he wanted to say floated silently across the space. *I love you all the more because of who you are.*

Chapter 13

Jake woke to the sounds of pots banging in the kitchen and soft feminine swearing. He turned to see Cheyenne at the stove and from the smells wafting through the small cabin, she was cooking something delicious.

He cautiously sat up, taking inventory of his aches and pains. His headache was gone but there was still a dull throbbing in his hand. He looked down at the bandage, wiggled his fingers and decided everything was good.

Which had him looking back at Cheyenne. She was dressed in a bright tee and white shorts, her feet bare. He wondered briefly where she had found clothes and then thought maybe he had been out of it longer than a night. Suddenly everything came back to him; her seductive treachery, the hateful words he had thrown in her face. Anger welled up in him again. Why was she still here? Hadn't he told her to get out of his life?

He must have made some sound, because she turned, giving him a tentative smile as she tucked her hair behind her ear. The movement drew his gaze to her orange shirt. *Caught on Lockabee Island* was stenciled in black with a picture of a fish behind bars.

Ha, he was the one who had been caught. He had known why she was here from the beginning, but as the days went by and they had gotten to know one another, it had become about them, not anything in Chicago. He had fallen under her spell, only to have her use their intimacy to try and trap him.

Swearing, he got up and went into the bathroom. The reflection in the mirror showed a pitiful specimen of man with unkempt hair, a bruise on one cheek and dark bristles covering his chin. He splashed water over his face and ran his fingers through his hair, only making it worse. What did it matter, he thought. It wasn't like he was trying to impress her. Not anymore. Without a word, he walked through the living room and out the door.

* * *

Cheyenne's heart sank as the door slammed behind Jake. She had known the minute she turned toward him that he had remembered everything that had happened, and he hadn't forgiven her.

143

But he kissed you last night, she told herself, yet knew it had been a kiss of compassion, not love. Slowly, she untied the towel she had worn as an apron, put a lid on the spaghetti sauce she had been simmering and shut off the stove.

Trevor had texted her about delays but he was on his way back. She would have him take her to town where she would pack her bag and catch the ferry to Red Haven. The hotels there were just fine for having a good cry while she waited for a flight back to Chicago.

Her lips trembled and she looked to the ceiling, willing the tears not to fall. She should never have let her guard down. She could have remained professional and insisted he remember she worked for his uncle. She should have continued to wear her suits to armor herself against the effect he had on her. She glanced down at the tee shirt Trevor had brought her from town and laughed humorlessly.

"Should have, would have, could have," she muttered, scooping up her favorite puppy from the box and going out onto the porch. Although all the dogs were Black Labs, this one, smaller than the rest, had a little patch of white on its chest. She hugged it close as she gazed around but didn't see any sign of Jake. Trevor's truck was still parked at the side of the cabin so he couldn't have gone far. She worried about his hand but he hadn't even given her time to check his bandage this morning.

"He's a big boy," she said to the puppy as she cuddled him. "He made his choices, both in Chicago and here, so he can just live with them." The puppy licked her trembling chin. "Oh, god," she moaned, burying her face in the soft fur and finally letting the tears flow because she knew that she would have to live with those choices, too, and her heart broke.

Minutes later Jake's Jeep came into view along the dirt road. Swiping her cheeks with the sleeve of her tee shirt, she tried to pull herself together as Trevor drove up. The puppy wiggled in her arms and she set it on the porch only to have it bound down the steps, tumbling over itself, to get to Trevor.

"Hey, mutt." He scooped the dog up and came to a stop at the edge of the porch. "Like the shirt," he quipped.

"I know Charlotte did not pick this out for me." She came down the steps to stand by him.

He grinned, then frowned when he looked at her more closely. "Where's Jake?"

She bit her lip to stop the trembling before she could answer. And then she could only shrug. "I hope you don't mind but I looked through your cupboards and found stuff to make spaghetti sauce."

"I never mind when I don't have to eat my own cooking."

"Hey!" The shout came from the tower, and they both turned to watch Jake hurrying down the ladder one handed. He slipped a rung and Cheyenne gasped. The fool man was set on killing himself. If he didn't she just might do it for him.

Running the short distance to where they stood, he stopped to catch his breath. Cheyenne flushed when she saw he held her black dress crushed against his chest.

"Hank said it was Max's Corsica with some unknown drivers following us," he gasped. "Apparently they followed the Jeep, even with you driving," he nodded toward Trevor, "because they're at the park entrance."

"Crap," Trevor swore. "I was cautious; I didn't think anyone was behind me."

Jake quickly pulled out his phone and tapped a contact. Cheyenne could only hear his part of the conversation, but it was quick and curt.

"I thought you would have found them by now. This island doesn't take thirty minutes to drive around." A pause, then he continued, "They're at the park entrance. We're going out the back way. You know where to find me." He hurried over to the Jeep to grab a backpack from the rear before coming back and grabbing Cheyenne's hand, pulling her toward the cabin.

"Come on. We have to get out of here."

She followed Jake inside and watched as he stuffed his blazer and her dress into the back pack. She picked up her heels; the ones she had worn to dinner what seemed like a lifetime ago. Had it only been two days?

"You can't walk out of here in those. Give them to me."

She clutched them to her chest. "First, and foremost, you are not tossing away another pair of my shoes. Second, have you forgotten you drove out here?"

"There's only one road into the park from the entrance off Highway 1. It ends at Mt. Baker. Traffic goes up and back on the same road."

Her heart skipped a beat. "So we can't get out of here without going past whoever is after you?"

He shook his head, grabbed her shoes and added them to the pack. When they exited the bedroom, Trevor handed Jake bottles of water and some snack bars then tossed him a tee shirt which he quickly pulled over his head.

"Let's go."

"Jake, I'm barefoot." It hadn't seemed like a big deal being without shoes in the cabin but she wasn't about to walk through the forest that way.

Trevor quickly went into the back room and came out with a pair of socks and tennis shoes that looked huge. "Take these."

"You'll need to buy Trevor another pair on the Donovan expense account." Jake's voice dripped sarcasm and Cheyenne sputtered.

"You expect me to wear those?" She stood with arms askew.

"What, they don't match your outfit?"

His rude words struck her like a blow, and something in her expression made him stop with a sigh. "Please. Put those on so we can get out of here."

Jake led her out the door but stopped and turned back to where Trevor stood in the doorway. "Thanks, man."

Trevor nodded. "I've got your back. If they get this far before the sheriff stops them, I can waylay them with park permits."

Jake turned toward a path into the woods. "Can you walk all right in those?" He asked as Cheyenne clopped beside him in shoes too large, even with two pairs of socks.

"I exercise; I can manage a few miles."

Not really wanting to tell her it was more like four miles, he took the lead down the narrow path and kept up a steady pace. Luckily the path was well marked. As he walked, he thought back to what he had seen from the ranger tower. She had been crying on the porch, and that sight had torn at his heart. From the first time he had kissed her, he knew he had found what was missing from his life. So why had he thrown it all away with his careless words without giving her a chance to explain? He was not one for dramatics. His uncle, and his mother, God rest her soul, had thrown enough hysterics to last him a lifetime yet he had certainly acted like the broken hearted hero in a Greek tragedy.

Cheyenne, on the other hand, had risen far and above any of them. After hearing her painful story, it was no wonder she was so loyal to his uncle. The prestige of her position at the Academy insured that people would respect her and she certainly deserved that, given what she had been through.

So why had he callously ruined the intimacy they had shared? Of all the people in the world to disrespect her, it should not have been him. He loved her.

He quickly glanced back to make sure Cheyenne was close then kept walking. He had a fuzzy memory of saying those words; but had it been out loud? Would she even believe him if he said it to her now?

The sun was setting by the time they reached the cottage and Jake knew he could not get her safely back to town tonight, even if the threat was gone. Yet how safe was she with him? He wanted her again with an ache that ran deep but knew there were issues between them to resolve.

He tossed the backpack in the corner and headed to the small kitchen area. "I'm afraid about all I have to eat is soup," he said as he opened one cupboard after another looking at his meager supplies.

"We would have had spaghetti if not for scurrying off through the forest."

He jaw dropped. "You made spaghetti? That was what I smelled?" His stomach grumbled in protest.

She shrugged. "There is so much you don't know about me..." She let the sentence trail off.

So you shouldn't have judged me, Jake mentally finished for her. *You should have trusted me.*

"I think I'll take a bath," Cheyenne said and hurried off to the bathroom. She shouldn't have been so harsh on him, but she honestly didn't know what to do; how to act. She couldn't imagine that he wanted her here, yet she was stuck, at least for the night until she could call Lindsay to pick her up.

As she soaked in the tub, she heard Jake moving around in the outer room, but it wasn't until she had gotten out that she realized she hadn't brought any clean clothes in with her. She wrapped in a towel and peeked out the door.

His gaze immediately found her. He quickly turned around and walked to the counter to plug in his phone. She glanced to where he had thrown the backpack but it was nowhere in sight. She made a dash into the bedroom, hoping he had put it there. She found the other outfit Trevor had gotten her laid out on the bed and quickly dressed.

When she moved over to the mirror to try and untangle her hair, she found her silver clip lying next to his comb. Her eye caught a sparkle in the closet and she sucked in a breath. Her black dress was neatly hung up beside Jake's blazer. Looking down, her heels were exactly lined up next to his loafers. She groaned. What did he want from her?

She heard a phone ring and knew she couldn't hide forever. When she came out of the bedroom, and Jake saw her, he moved the phone away from his ear and put it on speaker.

"Sheriff, what's up?"

"Max's Corsica was gone by the time I got to the park. It's dark so I must have missed them on the way there. I checked back at the Ferry port and the car was there but the men gone. I do know they're not staying on the island, so they must be ferrying back and forth."

"Did Max know their names; anything about them?"

"You know Max. He takes cash only and doesn't ask questions." The sheriff paused before adding, "Jake, why would someone be after you? You haven't been a resident long but you seem to belong. Is there something I need to be worried about?"

"George, I'm not hiding from the law if that's what you mean. I'm just an ordinary guy."

Cheyenne coughed.

"We both know who you are," the sheriff replied. "That's why I asked you to play at Ramsey's wedding. I only keep quiet about it as I don't want hordes of people capsizing the ferries trying to catch a peek at you."

Jake hadn't known. "I appreciate that." He hung up and turned back to her.

"Why is someone following us?"

"You're the famous one. I have nothing of value to anyone."

His gaze caressed her until she thought she would burst into flames. "You're wrong about that, Cat." His use of her nickname made her melt; his gaze sending signals that caused her heart to pound.

He reached for her and banged his injured hand against a chair.

"Shit." He cringed and clutched his hand against his chest, the moment shattered.

"Let me see." She hurried over as he collapsed in the chair. His bandage was dirty and had partly unraveled. "Do you have a first aid kit?"

"In the bathroom; under the sink," he said through clinched teeth.

She hurried to get it, coming back to find him with a bottle of whiskey on the table.

"Are you going to drink it or use it on your wound?" She took the bottle from him as he struggled to get it open. She went into the kitchen and got a glass, then easily twisted the cap open.

"Both," he grumbled. When she poured him a shot, he took the bottle from her and dumped more into the glass.

Cheyenne was surprised at how fast his mood had changed, although she couldn't blame him and was somewhat glad it had. They needed to talk although now didn't seem the time.

"Ouch. Damn." He jerked his hand back as she picked at the last layer of gauze.

"Drink." She waited as he raised the glass and took a swallow, grimacing. "More." The remaining gauze was bloody and she worried about what was beneath. Hurrying to the sink, she ran some warm water in a pan and brought it back to the table. She gently lowered his hand into it and he hissed.

When she looked up, he was staring at her. She thought that was better than him looking at the mess on his palm. "I'm sorry it hurts," she said softly.

"I'm sorry I hurt you."

She sucked in a breath, the words hanging in the air between them.

"Cheyenne?"

"Jake; don't." She bent her head to her work, blinking furiously to clear the tears so she could see his cut. She would think about what he said later. Not now. The water helped loosen the last of the gauze and she pulled it away. The gash was clean after the blood washed away, and although slightly pink, it didn't appear swollen or infected. He lifted his hand out of the water and patted it dry while she found the disinfectant and more gauze. Neither said a word, but the air crackled with tension.

She cleared away the mess and took the first aid kit back to the bathroom. When she returned, Jake was nowhere to be seen, and neither was the liquor bottle.

Chapter 14

Jake stayed on the back porch late into the night. He consumed a quantity of whiskey in the hope of drowning his sorrows, but he was still sober, which pissed him off so he drank even more. He had hoped his words would be an opening to get back in Cheyenne's good graces, but she would have none of it. How was he to tell her how he felt if she wouldn't listen? He laughed humorlessly. *Right back at you,* he thought, knowing he hadn't given her the chance to explain either.

An owl hooted and another answered. He heard sea gulls down by the dock and the gentle splash of waves as the tide came in. But nowhere in the darkness did he hear the answer to his question. The windows darkened behind him and he imagined her curled up in his bed and groaned. All his life, he had always gotten anything he wanted. If he hadn't bought it himself, other people had given him gifts; priceless and beautiful things that held no real value to him.

Now, the only thing he wanted, which was both beautiful and priceless, was slipping through his fingers and all his money, all his fame, could not keep that from happening. He looked into the inky night and a shooting star crossed the sky. He squeezed his eyes shut and repeated the childish wishing rhyme, ending with his wish. "I wish for one more chance to make it right."

* * *

Jake woke the next morning as the door clicked quietly closed. He panicked as he hurried to the front door, thinking Cheyenne had sneaked out before he had a chance to talk to her. Opening it quickly he looked all around but didn't see her.

Racing around the side of the house barefoot, his gaze shot to the dock and he stopped, sucking in a deep breath. She stood silhouetted against the sunrise, looking out to sea. Thank God she hadn't left. Even as small as Lockabee was, he knew she could disappear faster than he could find her. As he walked down the grassy slope, she picked up a small stone, flicked her wrist and threw it across the water. It dropped into the bay with a single plop. As he watched, she picked up another and tried again. The same thing happened.

"You have to flick your wrist just right," he said as he came up behind her. She turned swiftly and her eyes opened with surprise. "Here, let me show you."

He turned her back to face the water and stepped close behind her. Curling one arm around her waist, he took her other hand and stretched it out, showing her how to bring it around and flick it at the last moment. Her stone went skipping across the water. She gave a laugh. She had a rock in her other hand and now transferred it.

"Again."

"You can do it yourself. Just like you have all your life, Cheyenne."

Instead of throwing the rock, she turned in his arm. "Jake?"

He wrapped his other arm around her. "Sh. Listen to me. I was wrong; so wrong and I owe you the deepest of apologies."

She was shaking her head. "No. I shouldn't have asked you to go home. I'm the one who's sorry."

"You were doing your job."

"No. Nothing that has happened between you and me was about my job. Please believe that."

And he did. Swinging her around, he sank with her to the sand. Her kiss was wild and hungry and he answered her in kind. Her fingers threaded through his hair as she

152

held him close. When he finally came up for air, he saw tears in her eyes.

"What?"

She shook her head. "I watched you out the window last night, in the dark, and I saw a shooting star so I made a wish. It just came true."

He laughed; truly laughed for the first time in days. Dragging her to her feet, he pulled her up the grass.

"Where are we going?"

"There's no sense making love to you on the sand when we have a perfectly good bed in the cottage."

They never made it to the bed, at least not until later. The minute they were inside the door, he pulled her to a stop and tugged her shirt over her head. Her hands were frantic on him as she jerked down his shorts. She clung to him as he kissed her, his hands removing the rest of her clothes.

He groaned when they came together, her skin soft and hot against his. Hands roamed freely down her back and along her hips as he backed her cautiously across the room. It didn't matter that he misjudged the doorway and they bumped into the wall. She lifted a leg to wrap around his hips and he was lost.

Palming her fanny, he lifted her. She slid a hand between them and closed it around his erection, guiding him to her. He pushed up, impaling her and she lifted her other leg to lock them behind his waist.

Her fingers dug into his back. He nipped at the side of her neck and she threw her head back, silently urging him to further exploration. All the while, his hips pumped against hers.

"Faster," she ordered and it made him smile.

Instead of complying, he slowed his rhythm, watching her face as she became aware. Her heels pushed against the small of his back.

"Maybe I'm not ready for capriccio," he whispered against her lips. "I want the entire sonata and it must be in harmony."

"I love it when you talk dirty." She kissed him, her mouth hot and sweet against his and all the while he moved inside her.

Then her mouth was on his neck; sucking, biting.

"Jake, I'm begging you; please."

He pushed deep inside her; once, then again. She closed her eyes, pleasure racing across her features. He varied his rhythm until he couldn't have held back if the world stopped. And his gaze never left her. He knew the instant she was close; not from the tightening of her muscles around him but from the way her lips began to curve into a smile.

"You...are...so...beautiful," he breathed the words with each thrust of his hips. And then he couldn't speak at all as she climaxed around him and he hit the peak with her and flew over.

* * *

Cheyenne couldn't catch her breath and she could barely hold on as Jake kept her pressed against the wall. She dropped her head to his shoulder as the last tremors faded away.

"Never, ever in my life," she started but couldn't form a thought.

He kissed her ear and nibbled the lobe. "Me, too."

She started to unlock her legs but he griped her fanny tighter. "Don't move; not yet."

"You can't hold me up forever."

"I can try."

The mood was ruined when her stomach growled loud enough to be heard in town.

It made him laugh, which caused funny little tingles in her nether regions. She squeezed her inner muscles and he groaned.

"So unfair." He swatted her butt lightly and allowed her to slowly slide her feet to the floor. "I'd better feed you. I wouldn't want you to faint on me the next time." He left her and she leaned against the wall to watch him. He was

154

music in motion, muscles tightening and relaxing. She almost smacked her lips as he bent to pick up pieces of clothing. What a fine butt he had.

He fixed them soup and ham sandwiches then took her to bed. This time his lovemaking was slow and sensual, making her entire body ache with longing before he finished with her. She curled sleepily against his chest, his hand rubbing lazy circles on her back.

She fingered the bandage on his injured hand and he wiggled his fingers.

"Don't worry; they work." Though he tried to sound lighthearted, she sensed otherwise. Lifting her head, she saw him frown before his face cleared. "It'll be alright, Cat. I promise." He pushed her head back to his chest.

She fell asleep wondering what exactly would be all right – his hand, his relationship with his uncle, or his relationship with her. She sincerely hoped it wasn't one or the other.

* * *

"Cheyenne! Jake!" Pounding on the door woke her and she jerked upright.

"Oh, no. I forgot about Lindsay." She scrambled to untangle the sheets as Jake swung his feet to the floor and grabbed his shorts.

"What's she doing out here?" he asked.

"I called her this morning," Cheyenne said, then hesitantly added, "to come and get me."

Jake shot her a look, but was surprisingly calm when he said, "Stay here. I'll talk to her."

She sat huddled on the bed, listening to murmured voices past the partly open door. Within minutes, he was back. He stopped just inside the door, his gaze hot and fierce. He stalked toward her, slowly unbuttoning and unzipping his shorts and dropping them to the floor. He started crawling up the bed and she scooted back.

"What did you tell her?"

155

"I took care of it, Cat." She loved the sound of her name on his lips. She loved it even more when he circled one ankle with his hand and ever so slowly pulled her toward him until she was flat on her back. He straddled her legs and stretched out over her until his weight bore her down on the mattress.

"Now," he whispered as he kissed first one breast then the other. "I will take care of you."

When Cheyenne woke up a second time, Jake was no longer beside her. She called to him and when he didn't answer, she assumed he might be outside. She took a quick shower and threw on some clothes. She looked out the back window to see him down on the dock, so dug through the fridge for some cans of soda, grabbed a bag of chips she found on the counter, and hurried after him.

While she had showered, she thought about the limited number of days she had left before the deadline Donovan had given her. She wouldn't mention it again to Jake, because she realized that whatever happened between the two men, it was really out of her hands. What had her in a panic was that in that same number of days, she would have to say good bye to Jake.

She didn't know if she loved him. That term was not something that had been part of her life other than the love she felt for her sister. But she knew what she felt for Jake was more than the physical. He made her laugh and cry; caused anger and frustration, but she wouldn't have given up a minute of her time with him. So she decided to make the most of the time she did have.

"Hey, want a soda?" she asked as she walked to the end of the dock where he stood, fishing pole in hand.

"Sh, you'll scare the fish away." He held the rod with his right hand and tugged her close with the other.

"That's such a....fish tale." She laughed.

"How do you know? Have you ever asked a fish?"

"Well," she gave him a seductive smile. "I have been called a mermaid."

He kissed the tip of her nose. "More like a siren."

She pretended to pout. "I don't lure men to their deaths."

It was his turn to laugh. *"La petite mort."*

"Whoa!" He released her to grab the pole with both hands, then swore as it smacked against the gash on his palm. The tip of the rod dipped toward the water.

"You've got a bite!" she said excitedly.

"Here, take the pole. I can't hold it and reel in the line with this hand."

"I don't know what to do. I've never fished in my life."

"A first time for everything. I'll help you; I just can't handle the pressure against my hand." The pole bent again, the tip almost at the water.

She took the pole in both hands, feeling the power of the fish pulling at her. Jake stood at her back, giving her instructions. He held the pole steady with his good hand over hers, and showed her how lift the angle then reel in the slack.

"You've got it; keep it up."

She felt a sense of exhilaration when the fish leaped out of the water, but if Jake hadn't had an arm around her, she would most likely have fallen in the water. Once the fish, a Pacific Herring, Jake said, was close, he used the net to scoop it up.

"Dinner tonight," he said, carefully removing the hook. Cheyenne looked at the fish. It wasn't quite as large as it had looked in the water.

"One fish?" she asked and Jake laughed.

Kneeling on the dock he pulled up a stringer on which half dozen fish dangled and added hers to the clip. "Grab the pole and follow me. I'll show you how to gut and fillet them."

"I don't think so," she grimaced as they walked up the slope to the back porch. "Do you have any corn meal?"

He shrugged. "Probably."

"You do the fish and I'll see if you have what it takes for hush puppies."

He stopped in his tracks. "You really do cook?"

She smacked him on the arm. "Do not even start on me or I will burn your ears listing all my attributes."

He gave her a wolfish grin. "There's only one particular attribute I'm interested in."

They worked side by side in the little kitchen and Jake had never felt so content in his life. When he had first begun playing the piano, the music had carried him away; releasing any tension and making him forget any troubles. But it had been a one sided affair. He enjoyed the give and take with Cheyenne; loved making her laugh and laughing with her in return. It was a relationship where both of them were giving more than they took and he relished spending the rest of his life with her, whatever that life entailed.

He put the fillets on the grill while she made hush puppies and when everything was ready, he grabbed some beer from the fridge. They took their plates out on the porch to eat and watch the sun go down.

He reached for his beer and bumped his hand. Swearing, he pulled back and started to unwrap the bandage.

"Let me see it," Cheyenne said. He placed his hand in her outstretched one. "It doesn't appear to be swollen any more, nor is it red so I don't think it's infected. We really should get you in to the doctor just to be sure."

"I haven't heard anything from George, but we can't hide out indefinitely." He carefully turned his hand in hers, sliding up to circle her wrist. "While I would like to think we could live on sex, I'm afraid my stamina may deteriorate to the point where all I can do is lie on my back and let you do the work."

Cheyenne knew he was baiting her. She licked her lips and gave him her most seductive smile. "I have never been afraid of hard work."

He pulled, tugging her around the table and onto his lap. Laughing, she circled his neck and laid her head on his shoulder. His hand slid up her thigh to stop just under the hem of her shorts. That was all he seemed to need, for he gave a sigh and didn't move for the longest time. Together they watched the sky darken to deep purple, then a partial golden moon peeked over the horizon, its reflected light sparkling across the inky water. Soon it was full dark and a million stars twinkled above them.

"It's beautiful here," she said. "How did you ever find such a place?"

"I spun a globe, closed my eyes and put out my finger."

"Seriously?" She lifted her head enough to see his eyes glitter.

"Actually, the Washington coast has always held an appeal, but I didn't want a large city so I started looking at small, out of the mainstream islands."

"The better to hide."

He sighed. "I never meant it to be hiding. I simply needed to get away from everything and I couldn't do that while my mother…while she still needed me."

Cheyenne understood. "In a way, I did the same thing. I hated Sweetwater. It was small and dusty and I knew I had no future there. I hung on by a thread until Laramie graduated and then I took the first bus north."

"What about her? You didn't just leave her?"

"Of course not. She married her high school sweetheart and they are perfectly content. He ranches with his parents; cattle and horses and some such."

They lapsed into silence and it was so comfortable Cheyenne nearly went to sleep. She couldn't believe so much had happened in the past few days; ever since their dinner and car chase.

That made her sit up and wiggle around to face Jake.

"I have a question."

His eyes had been closed. Now, he opened one to peer at her. "Only one?"

She poked him in the chest. He caught her hand and held it against his heart and Cheyenne almost forgot what she had been thinking about. She could feel the steady beat beneath her fingers and longed to place a kiss right there. She placed one instead on his neck where the pulse throbbed. Immediately she felt his erection swell beneath her fanny.

"You'd better hurry," he said huskily.

"I was thinking about those guys chasing us and how we hid in the car wash."

"Okay." He slid his arm under her knees and started to get up.

"Wait. That wasn't the question."

"Leave it to you to be grammatically correct."

She kissed him lightly in appeasement. "I'm simply trying to make sure there has been adequate time since dinner before we…"

"We're not going swimming, Cat." He laughed. "I assure you if I get cramps it will be from holding back. You have ten seconds."

"Why is there a car wash on an island that doesn't allow cars?"

Well, that came out of nowhere, he thought. "We have cars."

She laughed. "Maybe twenty? Speaking of, how do you have one? You're not exactly a life-long resident."

"It came with the cottage and there's probably more than twenty, but from what I've heard some fifty years ago, cars were allowed on the island. People would drive around all day seeing the sights, park on the sand but the salt air would settle on them, causing rust if it wasn't washed off frequently. Hank took a notion to washing cars by hand down at the ferry port as people waited to leave. Over the years he made a ton of money and had just built the auto wash before the island council decided to only allow resident cars on the island."

"How unfair for him."

Jake shrugged. "But better for the island. There is less air pollution; the need for fewer gas stations which preserves the landscape and fewer accidents for a two man police force to handle. Plus it was the incentive for other businesses to spring up – bicycle rentals and repairs and the rickshaw taxis."

"So they sacrificed one for the good of many," she said defensively.

"No one was sacrificed. This isn't *Survivor*. Every car owner on the island probably gets their car washed once a week at Hank's."

"That hardly makes a living wage."

"Why are you defending the man? You only met him once."

She gave him a cheeky grin and said, "I liked him. No one has ever called me a *looker* before."

He laughed. "Your ten seconds are up." With that, he scooped her up and headed for the cottage, his voice dropping to a sexy drawl. "Hank said he had good eyesight. I would say he's right."

Chapter 15

Cheyenne woke to the smell of coffee. When she wandered out of the bedroom, Jake's gaze immediately found hers and he smiled as though he had just gotten his favorite toy for Christmas. She returned the smile with a grin. She had definitely gotten an early Christmas present; actually more than one and she blushed in memory.

"Where did you get that shirt, by the way?"

Cheyenne looked down. "Trevor bought it for me."

"And you complained about the hats I picked out?"

She took the cup of coffee he handed her. "Neither of you have any fashion sense, but if you recall, all I had was that black dress."

"In which you looked totally sexy, by the way. You'll have to wear it again sometime." He paused as he scooped scrambled eggs onto a couple of blue speckled tin plates. "So I can get you out of it again." He had handed her a plate and she almost dropped it at his suggestion. "Don't you dare drop that. It was the last of the eggs and until Lindsay gets here, we're going to be living on beer."

As though by magic, or telepathy, there was a knock at the door. Jake, bare chested and sexily indecent, went to answer it as Cheyenne raced back into the bedroom for her shorts. When she immerged, Lindsay was pulling in her suitcase and Jake followed her with two bags of groceries. Cheyenne started to speak but never got a chance.

"Girl, you are the talk of the town!" Making herself perfectly at home, Lindsay went to the kitchen and poured a cup of coffee.

Cheyenne collapsed into a chair. "Why?" she asked weakly although she wasn't sure she wanted to know.

"Are you going to eat those?" She pointed to the plate of eggs.

Cheyenne's stomach was too full of butterflies to think about putting eggs in it. She pushed the plate toward Lindsay.

"What's going on?" Jake asked, head in the fridge as he deposited milk, more eggs, meat and beer and shut the door.

"Well, first everybody knows you two have been seeing one another, but now we have Trevor Sycamore buying you clothes," Lindsay pointed at her with the fork, "and Trevor is in a relationship with Charlotte."

"But Charlotte knew why he was doing that," Cheyenne tried to defend herself.

"Yes, but that doesn't put the brakes on the gossip wheels. Especially when *I* then get your clothes and check you out of the Inn with Mrs. Godfrey."

"You checked me out?" she asked but her gaze was on Jake. He gave her an innocent grin. "Wait. You didn't tell Mrs. Godfrey where I was, did you?"

"No, but that's why there's so much gossip. You, me, Charlotte, Trevor, Jake; it's a kinky little five-some so everyone is speculating."

Cheyenne covered her face with her hands.

"Everyone?" The last thing in the world Cheyenne had ever wanted was gossip, even knowing it would most likely never reach Chicago.

"This is Lockabee," Jake and Lindsay said in unison.

Cheyenne didn't have time to stew before Jake asked, "Is there any talk about those strangers who were following us?"

"How would she know about that?" Cheyenne asked.

Lindsay and Jake both looked at her.

"Never mind."

"I didn't hear anything but you might call Sheriff Franklin."

"We should go into town," Jake said.

"I'd take you but I have some passengers waiting for a ride back to town from East Bay." Lindsay finished her coffee and stood.

"I'll drive," Jake said.

Her brows rose. "I didn't see your car outside. Going to take the boat?"

"Damn. I forgot it's at Trevor's. I'll have to get him to come pick us up."

Jake went into the bedroom and came out with some cash which he pressed into Lindsay's hand. "Thanks for getting the groceries."

"And my clothes," Cheyenne added. "You did get my computer, too, didn't you?"

"Everything's present and accounted for. Mrs. Godfrey said she had your credit card on file so you're good with her."

Jake saw Lindsay out and Cheyenne dug through her bag. Pulling out a cord, she plugged in her phone, which had died yesterday and she hadn't been able to charge it with Jake's charger.

"What are you doing?" he asked when he came back.

"Seeing if I still have a job." She looked at him. "I haven't checked in or been on line in days."

He didn't say anything but his look spoke volumes. Neither of them wanted to mention the inevitable; time was running out.

"I'm taking a shower."

As soon as the battery showed any life, Cheyenne checked her messages. To her surprise there were none. Was Mr. Donovan so mad at her for not checking in that he wasn't even bothering to call? She booted up her computer and once again, nothing was new since the last time she had worked.

She quickly punched in the number she needed, but instead of Mr. Donovan, a female answered whose voice she didn't recognize.

"Mr. Donovan, please."

"I'm sorry; he can't come to the phone."

Cheyenne paused, then took the plunge. "This is his executive assistant, Cheyenne Tucker."

"Oh." The voice was startled, then hesitant. "Miss Tucker, do you have news?" There was coughing and grumbling in the background.

"Well, no," she replied, "but I—"

"Good bye." The call disconnected.

Cheyenne stared at the phone in her hand. Had that been Mr. Donovan she heard in the background? Why wouldn't he have spoken to her?

She looked toward the bathroom where she still heard the sound of water. Knowing there was nothing she could do for the moment, she quietly opened the door, steaming rushing to meet her.

"One thing about it, this place has a huge hot water heater." Jake poked his head around the curtain. "But it doesn't hurt to conserve."

Shaking off the foreboding she had felt over her phone call, she stripped quickly and stepped into the tub under the spray. She turned her back and rubbed against Jake's soapy chest and he brought his hands up to cup her breasts. Her senses were immediately overwhelmed.

He turned her toward him, bending to capture a breast in his mouth. His hands slid down her belly and his long fingers sought her center. She in turn circled him, squeezing as her hand slid down the length of him and back up.

"Love me," he whispered as he lifted her leg and she guided him to her.

And she suddenly realized that she did love him. She loved him because he saw her and accepted her for who she was. His tender lovemaking left her aching. She didn't care if he lived like a beach bum on a little island in the middle of nowhere; she wanted to be there with him.

As he took her to the crest and they crashed over together, she knew that for now, her secret would remain locked in her heart. There were things that needed to be

165

resolved and she only hoped they could be, before it was too late.

Their love play continued even after their initial thirst was quenched. He lathered his hands and washed her, lingering on her sensitive breasts. She soaped his hair and kissed him while scrubbing until bubbles got in her eyes. Laughing they stood under the spray until the water ran cold, then toweled off and raced for the bed.

Much later, he caressed her midriff before planting a kiss on her belly button.

"You've become my muse," he said. "I dream of you; of your smile and your hair; your graceful walk and your long legs." As he spoke, he kissed his way down one of the aforementioned limbs, tickled her toes with his tongue, then kissed his way back up.

"You are the melody I hear in my head every waking moment."

She didn't know what to say to his elegant words but he didn't seem to need a response. His head rested on her chest, the hand caressing her stomach finally stilled. As he slept, tears silently seeped from her eyes as she whispered, "I love you, Jake Smith, with my heart and soul. I just pray to God it will be enough."

* * *

"Hey, get up. Trevor will be here in ten minutes." Jake grabbed Cheyenne's foot and began dragging her to the end of the bed. She stretched, arms high overhead, and the sheet slipped dangerously low. He groaned. If he had a choice, he would spend his life in bed with her. She gave herself freely. She had brought laughter into his life at a time where he had reached his lowest and he didn't know what he would do without her.

Then tell her, he lectured himself. *You still have time.* But did he? He knew enough about Cheyenne to know she had ethics among other lovely attributes. That and her sense of responsibility toward his uncle would mean in less than a week, he would have to make a decision.

"Come on; rise and shine."

She brushed the hair out of her eyes. "We did not sleep the day and night away; did we?"

"No, it's only three but I want to get into town before Doc closes up shop."

She scrambled to the end of the bed and grabbed his hand. "Is it infected? Did it split open?" Her hair fell forward as she examined his palm and he gathered a clump with his free hand and gently raised her head.

"It's fine." He kissed her on the forehead. "I want to see how long the stitches should stay in."

"Trevor didn't exactly sew a straight line, did he?" She tenderly traced the jagged path of the gash with her finger.

It still amazed him how the prickly Miss Tucker had so completely disappeared, to be replaced by the compassionate and affectionate Cheyenne. Sometimes Jake wondered if the former had ever really existed.

"It'll give me something to talk about over beer with the boys."

"You are such a guy." She shook her head, climbing out of bed and digging through her suitcase on the floor for clothes. He closed his eyes and groaned. Oblivious to what she was doing to him with her sassy ass in the air, she straightened, pulling on a pair of bikini briefs.

"We really need to do laundry." She agilely hooked her bra and tugged on a top, then shorts.

He had never done laundry in his life. Her comment was so…ordinary. The fact that she hadn't commented, discussed terms or made demands when he said she would stay with him was so…ordinary. Like two old married people planning their day. His mouth turned dry as he watched her pull her hair into a ponytail and don the mermaid hat he had bought her. Were all the planets in the solar system aligning in order to give him this one chance at happiness?

"Jake? I asked if you had a basket or something we can use to carry these clothes."

"Are you trying to domesticate me?"

She sighed and gave him a look that was pure Miss Tucker. "I am trying to make sure you don't smell." She walked out of the room with an armful of clothes. "Strip the bed and grab the towels. We might as well do it all."

He grinned. He didn't mind at all that she was bossing him around. He knew exactly how to get back at her. He sneaked up behind and grabbed her, making her squeal. He turned her toward him, his head descending to kiss her when Trevor knocked and let himself in.

"Hey, buddy. How's the hand?" He looked from one of them to the other and stood there grinning.

"Two fingers fell off last night, but other than that, fine." Jake wished everyone would quit worrying about him. He was not a wuss. He had found himself quite capable these last months on the island and liked who he had become – his own man.

"Ignore him," Cheyenne said. "He hasn't been in a fight for over three days and is grouchy."

"Ouch," Trevor laughed.

They stuffed their laundry in all the available canvas grocery bags, loaded it in the back of the Jeep and headed to town, dropping Trevor back at the Ranger station. The summer heat had found its way to the island, and even with the breeze coming in off shore, the sun showed no mercy. As they drove past Inland Bay, the beach looked like a field of wildflowers – colored umbrellas, beach towels and sun bathers covered the sand. Swimmers bobbed in the shallows.

"Do you have a swim suit?"

Cheyenne had been looking out the window but now turned toward him. "I didn't exactly come here on vacation."

"Okay; no suit. I'll simply have to find a place to take you swimming where you don't need one."

She reached over and slowly slid her hand up and caressed the back of his neck. As he put the Jeep in park in front of the jail, she tugged him toward her.

"I'd like that," she whispered against his lips then kissed him. "A lot."

She got out of the Jeep but Jake couldn't move for several minutes, waiting for the discomfort to subside. Damn, she played dirty.

And he loved it.

Cheyenne was already talking to Sheriff Franklin when he entered the building. Seeing Jake, he waved him into the office.

"How's the hand?"

"Don't ask him that. He's like that story about a lion with a sticker in his paw." Cheyenne answered for him.

Sheriff cleared his throat before continuing. "You did a good job, according to Trevor. Given your former profession, I must say I'm impressed."

Jake decided not to take the comment personally. There was always talk that anyone in the classical music industry, as versus rock bands and country music stars, was effeminate. Instead, he changed the subject.

"Have you found anything new about our chasers?"

The sheriff shook his head. "I check with Max every day and no strange man duo has rented his car since that one day. He can't recall what they looked like; you two didn't see them, so there's not much to go on. The Prince Hotel is full, but I have no probable cause to get their guest list to run makes on all the guests."

Jake sighed. Everything he said was true, but it didn't sit right. There had to be a reason they were followed, and he had the feeling it wasn't over. Whatever "it" was.

He stood, putting out his hand. "Thanks for looking out for us. You have my number if anything comes up."

The sheriff walked out with them, commented on the heat, and left them at the door of the air conditioned building. The doctor's office was close, so they walked quickly down the block.

Doctor Stephens was in his early seventies, and as spry as anyone in their fifties. He still practiced part time in Red Haven, but spent the rest of his time on island, helping whenever he was needed. His full head of white hair lifted when the nurse escorted them in and he stood from behind his desk with a smile.

"I hear Sycamore is trying to put me out of business," he laughed as he shook Jake's hand.

"I doubt that will happen, given how he mutilated me."

"He did not." Cheyenne immediately defended his friend.

"This is Cheyenne Tucker," Jake said by way of introduction.

The doctor turned to her, curiosity then recognition lighting his blue eyes. "Ah, you're the young woman I've been hearing about."

"No," Cheyenne said quickly. "That must be someone else."

Jake shook his head. "She's joking. She's still getting used to being seen with me."

The doctor shook his head. "I must be getting old. I don't understand you young people anymore. Sit down and let me see what the damage is."

Jake sat, pulling Cheyenne down in the chair beside him and held out his hand. While the doctor examined his stitches, he studied her. She was biting her bottom lip, one foot was tapping nervously on the floor which made her knee bounce, and she was twisting her fingers together. He reached over and put his hand over hers. When she looked up, he gave her his best smile.

"Ouch." He turned back as the doctor probed the gash. Whatever Cheyenne's problem, now wasn't the time to talk about it.

"Still tender, hum? How long ago did this happen?"

"Four days," Cheyenne answered, which was good because Jake was still a little fuzzy about time passage after the fire.

"Trevor did a credible job, given how jagged the tear was. Move your thumb and fingers for me."

Jake did as asked, feeling a twinge and pull but no pain.

"It seems to be healing nicely but we'd better leave those stitches in another four, five days. How long has it been since you had a tetanus shot?"

"Probably the first week I was here when I stepped on a rusty can in the bay."

"Oh, right. That's good. I'll give you some salve. Those stitches will begin to pull as it heals and the salve will keep the skin soft."

He thanked the doctor, settled up with the receptionist and walked Cheyenne out into the heat. When she started toward the Jeep, he pulled her into the shade of a curbside tree.

"What's going on?" He tilted back her hat so he could read her eyes. She started to bite her lip again but he put his thumb up to stop her. "I'm the only one who can bite those gorgeous lips." His comment got a tentative smile.

"Jake, everyone knows you're hanging out with me. Doesn't that bother you?"

"No, why should it?"

"People know I'm not a resident; that I came here to find Joseph Donovan. It would be easy enough for anyone to figure out who I work for. What if someone puts two and two together and discovers *you* are Joseph Donovan? Your cover will be blown."

He laughed and hugged her tight. "You are irresistible." When she started to protest, he shushed her with a light kiss. "It's not *Mission: Impossible*," he said, then added, "Although I think I would prefer being James Bond."

She *tsked* him. "You're wrong about one thing. You are impossible." She gave a sigh as though accepting her fate. "As long as we're here, then, where's the Laundromat?"

They parked the Jeep in the small lot behind the local Laundromat. When he started to stick everything in one washer, Cheyenne pushed him aside and told him to get change from the machine and buy some soap packets. There was something very intimate about watching her put his briefs in with her bras and panties.

"Now what?" he asked as she put the quarters for the last load into the receptacle.

"You honestly have never done laundry? How have you managed in the past two months?"

He was almost embarrassed to say. "Mrs. Gilbert over there," he nodded his head, "was kind enough to do it for me after the first time I came in."

"Most likely because you tried to dump it all together?"

"It all needed washed."

The lady in question had trundled over to where they stood. "Hello, there, Jake, you dear boy." Mrs. Gilbert had to be going on ninety, used a walker to help her get around but everyday she came over from her house next door to monitor her business.

He bent to kiss her weathered cheek. "You are looking as lovely as ever, ma'am."

"Don't try and sweet talk me; I can see I'm being replaced." She looked Cheyenne up and down. "Can't say as I blame you. She's as pretty as everyone's been saying."

Jake heard Cheyenne groan.

Mrs. Gilbert turned to Cheyenne. "I swear this boy didn't know up from down the first time he came in. You'd think he'd grown up with servants; mixing his colors with whites; not knowing how to even properly fold a towel."

Jake watched Cheyenne's lips twitch and he slightly shook his head from behind the petite woman.

"Mrs. Gilbert, are you going to be here for awhile?" he asked.

"You know I will be. I have to keep an eye on those folks coming in with half the beach wrapped up in their towels. You just can't imagine what sand does to these washers." She shook her head in obvious dismay.

"Can I leave you some money to transfer our clothes to the dryers?"

"Well, now," she hesitated.

"I'll bring you some éclairs from the bakery."

She gave a dramatic sigh. "I suppose, since you are no longer on the market, I'll have to settle for something else sweet."

172

Cheyenne had a sudden fit of coughing and headed for the front door.

"You're a doll," he told Mrs. Gilbert and rushed after her.

He found her doubled over laughing. She straightened up, caught sight of him and started all over again.

"It's not that funny." He frowned slightly.

"You are such a...a troll," she exclaimed.

He wasn't sure that was a good thing, until she cupped his cheeks with both hands and kissed him.

"Have you beguiled everyone in this town?" she asked.

"Only the pretty ones," he replied with a smile. "Come on. We might as well eat since we have to wait for the sheets to dry and make the bed before I can beguile you."

She hooked her arm in his to walk down the street. "Oh, believe me; I am already captivated by your charm."

Chapter 16

Since the Laundromat was on Main Street, it didn't surprise Cheyenne when Jake steered her in the direction of Brenda Kay's.

"Hey, kiddos," the friendly proprietor said as they came through the door. At this time of day, the place was almost empty but Jake still took a booth at the back. Brenda sat their water glasses on the table. "Haven't seen the two of you in awhile. I heard there'd been some ruckus or the other out at the state park and from the looks of it," she nodded at Jake's hand, "I see the gossip was right."

She turned to Cheyenne with a wink. "Can't you keep him out of trouble?"

Cheyenne shook her head. "I'm afraid he's beyond redemption."

"I'm right here," Jake said. "I can hear you."

"Beer?" Brenda asked with a grin.

"Please," Cheyenne replied.

"Make it two; along with fish and chips."

"No," Cheyenne countered. "I want a big juicy hamburger; medium rare." At his look, she shrugged. "I need red meat."

Brenda placed their order and brought back their beer and some napkins. "I've got to run in a few. Kenny, my grandson is playing baseball tonight. Did you play as a kid, Jake?"

Jake pursed his lips for just a moment, but Cheyenne caught the hesitation. She reached over and laid her hand on his in support.

"Nope, never had the chance," he said flippantly. "How old is Kenny?"

"Only seven," Brenda replied. "You should see those little ones. They swing like they were chopping down a tree and their little legs get a-going when they run. They're a hoot."

The bell over the door rang and Brenda was off to seat a family of six. Cheyenne watched the merry band as they laughed and jostled each other and realized how much she missed her sister. Once this was over, and her heart twisted at that thought, she would make a trip to Sweetwater.

A movement past that family caught her eye and she noticed a man at a table by the door staring at her. She turned her head toward Jake and tried to look out of the corner of her eye but it didn't work.

"Let me see your sunglasses," she said and Jake passed them to her. She put them on, knowing the mirrored lenses would conceal her eye movements. Yes, one man was staring at her. When he spoke to his companion, that man also turned around and stared.

"It's not exactly bright in here," Jake said, a quizzical expression on his face.

She didn't answer but turned her head this way and that so she could watch the two men without appearing to stare. The larger of the two appeared quite agitated; pointing to his phone as he shared something with the other.

As Brenda brought out their meals, Cheyenne returned his glasses, leaning across the table to whisper, "Don't look, but there's two men over by the door who keep staring at me." When both Brenda and Jake started to turn their heads she hissed, "Don't look!"

"What do they look like?" Jake asked, casually picking up his beer. Brenda stayed rooted in place, whether out of fear that something was about to happen or in anticipation of the same, Cheyenne didn't know.

"One large, one small. Both have brown hair, dark shirts and pants, no hats. The small one has ears that seem to stick out. It's the bigger man who has a phone and keeps pointing at it while he's staring our way."

"They're definitely tourists if they're wearing dark clothes," Brenda scoffed. "Nobody in their right minds would wear that when it's ninety-five degrees out."

Cheyenne watched Jake struggle not to turn around and return the men's stares. From his expression, she knew he was thinking the same thing she was. These were the men who had followed them from the harbor restaurant days ago. Another quick glance their way and she had a very clear revelation. She gasped. "I'd swear they're the same two I saw at the Gold Pelican the first time I met you."

"We need to get out of here," he said to her then turned slightly to Brenda. "If you'll create a diversion, we'll slip out through the kitchen. Then call Sheriff Franklin and have him drop by and get a look at those two. They're not doing anything wrong, but that doesn't mean they aren't thinking about it."

Brenda nodded, went and grabbed a water pitcher and headed for that table. Cheyenne and Jake barely got their food rewrapped before a yelp and childish laughter had them glancing toward the front before hurrying out of the booth and slipping into the kitchen. The larger of the men had jumped out of his seat and was wiping down his front with a napkin as Brenda mopped at the water all over the table.

Dusk was falling as they hurried along the alley. Jake shoved his meal at her. "Get to the Jeep; I'll only be a minute." Cheyenne didn't question him, dropping into the seat as he appeared out a door with their canvas sacks of clothes. There was no back road out of town to the cottage, so they drove as fast as they dared once they got out of the city limits. Jake slowed down after the first mile when no one followed them.

Jake carried the clothes into the house and Cheyenne followed with their meals, for once happy that Brenda Kay served food wrapped up in brown paper instead of on a plate.

"Want another beer?" Jake said, head in the fridge.

"Sure. I need something to settle my nerves." At that moment, thunder cracked and a streak of lightning flashed low across the bay. She jumped a foot. "Damn. Where did that come from?"

Jake frowned as he opened the back door and looked out. Cheyenne could hear the wind rushing past the opening. "I should have known there was a storm brewing," he said as he forced the door closed again. "It was too dark for seven o'clock, but I never even looked up. I was more concerned about getting us out of there."

He came back with the beer and they sat at the table and ate as rain battered the roof and windows. When she caught him staring at her without saying anything, she said, "What is it?"

"Those men didn't see me; you said they were staring at you. While I readily admit you're a damned sight prettier than me, why would they be interested in you?"

"And looking for something on their phone."

Jake's gaze narrowed. "Or maybe looking at it." He pulled out his phone and tapped some icons, scrolled, then frowned. He turned it to show her.

"Oh, god." Her picture, larger than life, jumped out at her. Below was her title at Donovan Academy of Music. He scrolled down to his own picture.

"It wouldn't take a genius to connect us."

Cheyenne tried to deny his assumption. "You don't look anything like your picture on the website. How could they possibly...?"

"It really doesn't make any difference who they're after, if they're after us at all and we're not simply being paranoid. We're in it together, which means you need to stick to me like glue so I can protect you."

Cheyenne had been self sufficient since the age of sixteen; probably even earlier and the thought that she needed protecting should have rankled. Instead, her heart fluttered and warmth spread through her at the idea that

Jake cared enough to want to protect her. She jumped as another crack of thunder rattled the window panes.

"There's only one thing to do when it's pouring like this," Jake said as he collected their trash and bottles.

"I am not going walking in the rain." Cheyenne shook her head.

He came over and pulled her from her chair, circling her waist and gathering her close.

"Not what I was thinking," he whispered in her ear as he rubbed his hips against hers and she felt the evidence of what he had in mind.

"I'm not doing that in the rain either," she said.

"It would be like making love in the shower." He was kissing her neck and behind her ear, all the sensitive spots he could reach. Another boom and light flashed outside the window.

"Uh-uh. I have no interest in being struck by lightning and found naked on the deck."

Her comment made him chuckle and with a sigh he released her. "I guess we'll have to do this the old fashioned way; on a bear-skin rug in front of a fire."

"You have no bear-skin rug," Cheyenne said, sitting on the small table in front of the sofa as he put kindling and some wadded up paper in the small fireplace and lit a match. He looked over his shoulder, his gaze as hot as the cheery blaze he started.

"Use your imagination," he said as he pulled her down with him onto the braided rug.

It wasn't long before Jake's inventiveness far outran anything her imagination could conjure.

* * *

Jake loved making love with Cheyenne. He loved the feel of her skin; her womanly scent; the little sighs and breathy gasps that fluttered in the air between them as they explored each other.

"I adore you," he whispered against her stomach as he made his way up her body, leaving hot kisses across her hips; in the valley between her breasts, at the curve of her graceful neck.

"Mmm," she murmured languidly and he smiled, knowing he had thoroughly exhausted her. He, by contrast, felt energized. He quietly slid away, careful not to disturb her, and closed the door to the bedroom behind him. The storm still raged; rain pouring down the windows in sheets. Music again hummed through him, as it always did when he was with her, and he grabbed the score sheets he kept by the bed and started jotting down the notes. The piano solo was emotional and seductive; the background orchestra portions representing the fury of the storm. The entire piece was almost complete, although he would have to take it to a proper piano to get the full sound.

And it suddenly struck him that although it was good; in fact probably his best work ever, he could see evidence of his uncle throughout the score. In all honesty he did have much to be grateful for where his uncle was concerned as the man had given him the foundation on which he had built his career. It had only been in later years that he had become impossible. His thoughts were confusing, but he remained firm about the fact that he had not composed any of this for his uncle.

He had told himself he wouldn't enter a competition again and the fact was he hadn't composed even a single phrase since his mother had died. But Cheyenne had inspired him; invigorated him and made him want to compose.

He smiled. Okay, so he wanted to impress her. In doing so, he would also be doing what his uncle wanted, although Jake didn't plan on telling him. He put another sequence of chords on the score and set it aside as the bedroom door creaked open.

"Why didn't you wake me?" Cheyenne stretched her arms over her head and Jake reacted immediately. Her breasts rose, the tips peaking as she stood in all her naked glory; a picture of beauty framed by the rough wood of the door.

"Come here," he growled, swinging his legs onto the bed and leaning against the headboard.

Her hips swayed as she sauntered slowly to the end of the bed. Like a wild cat on the prowl, she slowly crawled over him, stopping to kiss his knees. He sucked in a breath. He had done the same to her, never realizing how erotic the action was. She looked up at him through her hair and grinned before continuing her explorations, each kiss higher and higher.

"Cat." He threaded his fingers through her hair; watching; anticipating her next move but he still wasn't prepared for the shock when she bit his hip. He jerked and heat shot through him. Pure sensation flooded his brain and it took extreme effort to hold still. That lasted for no more than an eight count as she continued her explorations.

"Stop." He circled her arms and lifted her up to kiss her pouting lips. His hands cupped her breasts; thumb and forefinger pinching her nipples until they pebbled, all the while tongues dueled and moans echoed the thunder still rumbling outside.

"Jake." She pulled back, gasping. "You make me ache." She rubbed against his belly, her fanny pressing back against his erection. Her breasts bobbed and he couldn't resist sucking one into his mouth.

"Now."

He grinned at her command which reminded him so much of the unyielding Miss Tucker. But it was the intrepid, sultry Cat whose hot sheath was slowly taking him in. Her blue gaze enticed him; her sexy sigh seduced him as she ground against him. And then she stopped.

He released her breast and raised his head to watch her eyes close. Pink tongue peeked between lush lips; nostrils flared as her inner muscles squeezed him; once; then again.

When she opened her eyes and found him watching her, she smiled almost shyly. "You are so very fine, Jake Smith," she said as she ran her fingers through his hair and clasped them behind his head. Pulling him forward she kissed him and he savored the taste of her.

And then she began to move. Cymbals crashed and drums rolled in a rhythm that was indefinable and yet intuitive. He spread his hands across her bottom and her knees clinched him tighter. The tempo sped up and she jerked her head back, gasping. He sucked her neck, the sensitive curve of her breast and still she rocked against him until as one, they exploded. For every spasm of his orgasm, she squeezed him tighter in her own release. When they finally drifted back to earth, she collapsed against his chest. His arms fell to the side, too weak to even hold her.

After long minutes where all he heard was their harsh breathing, he felt her shudder against him.

"Are you all right?" he managed to say.

She shook her head slightly but he was sure he heard a sound. He lifted her off his chest so he could see her face and she burst into a fit of giggles.

"Should I be offended?"

She shook her head again, pressing her lips together but her mirth still showed in her glittering gaze. When she finally managed to contain herself, she bent forward and quickly kissed him.

"Did you hear music?" she asked. "I swore I heard music at the very moment…"

She didn't need to finish. If he hadn't already loved her, he would have fallen at that moment, knowing their hearts were so in tune with each other.

* * *

Cheyenne work the next morning to Jake's voice in the outer room. She quickly pulled on his tee shirt and peeked out the bedroom door, assuring herself he was on the phone and not taking to a visitor. He walked out the back door as she poured a cup of coffee and hung up just as she joined him on the porch.

"That was Trevor. He wanted to know if I was still alive and kicking." He took her cup and sipped the coffee.

"And then some," she replied as he pulled her close with his other arm and kissed her.

181

"Oh, yeah." He started to kiss her again but his phone rang. "It's Franklin." He pushed the call button and put it on speaker. "What's up, Sheriff?"

"I got to Brenda's but those men had left. Seems they didn't like her service." The sheriff laughed. "I didn't see them on the street but she gave me a description and I took prints off their water glasses. Trouble is, I don't have the software to run them here, so will have to get them to Seattle and that'll take awhile. Even so, they haven't done anything wrong at this point."

"I know," Jake said. "We have no idea if it's just a coincidence or if they're after something."

"Well, all we can do is keep an eye out. Oh, and by the way, I've been checking and they're not renting Max's car. That's one less way we have of tracking them so you be careful out there."

"Will do." Jake disconnected with a sigh.

"Now what?" Cheyenne asked.

He hugged her. "Nothing to do but wait until he hears something. Like I told him, we don't even know for sure what they're up to. Maybe they were simply admiring a pretty face."

Cheyenne didn't believe him, and from the look on his face, he didn't believe his own words.

"We'll just have to lay low for a few days."

Cheyenne found Jake's idea of lying low in a secluded cottage by a bay meant swimming naked in the moonlight and making love under the stars. They took long walks in the forest, one day ending up at the Ranger station where Cheyenne played with the puppies and the guys drank beer and told her outrageous stories of their fishing exploits. Yet her favorite memory of those days was when they cuddled in a blanket one morning to watch the sun rise over crystal water. Neither spoke of the time slipping away.

On the third day of their self-imposed solitude, the sheriff called again.

"It seems those two have been spotted around town asking about Joseph Donovan," he said, static through the speaker making it hard for her to understand most of what he said. She did clearly hear *Joseph Donovan* and her heart skipped a beat.

"Asking who?" Jake replied.

"Well, so far I've heard from Brenda Kay, Lindsay, Mrs. Gilbert at the Laundromat, and McNally down at the harbor."

"Crap," Jake swore.

Cheyenne had to wonder if everyone on the island knew who Jake really was. If so, it was the worst and best kept secret at the same time.

"You know what, Sheriff? Maybe we should let them catch me," Jake said, a gleam in his eye.

"No," she whispered fiercely.

"Absolutely not," the sheriff replied at the same time.

He caught her hand and held her still when she tried to storm off the deck. His gaze locked with hers as he continued talking to the sheriff. "Look. We know they're looking for me, but they don't know we know, so we bait them."

Cheyenne vehemently shook her head, her eyes tearing. She mentally cursed the Sheriff when he agreed with what Jake was suggesting.

"That might work, if you try it in a public place where I can keep an eye on you and have my deputy as backup. What are you thinking?"

"I need to visit Dr. Stephens and get my stitches out." He looked at his watch. "Give us two hours and then we'll be at the Gold Pelican."

Chapter 17

Cheyenne argued with him all the way to town, but he refused to listen.

"I can't live looking over my shoulder all the time." He tried to sound patient. "If my uncle didn't send them, they're after something else. Either way, I need to find out."

"But there are two of them."

"And Cam, the sheriff and a deputy will have my back."

She pursed her lips and turned to look out the window, ignoring him the rest of the trip.

Jake knew she didn't understand his need to be independent. And to tell the truth he was a little worried, even if he felt he was capable of taking care of himself. He had always had security while on tour so the paparazzi never got close. And he had the feeling these guys weren't looking to take photographs or they wouldn't be acting so suspicious.

He exited the doctor's office with a simple elastic wrap, his hand none the worse although the scar was still somewhat pink and tender. When Cheyenne walked away without a word, he quickly caught up and hooked an arm around her waist. Although stiff as a board, she did stop.

"Hey." He stepped in front of her and lifted her chin with a finger. Her gaze flitted here and there. "Look at me." With a sigh, she finally met his gaze.

"Can't you trust me?" His question went far beyond an encounter at the bar and he knew she realized it.

Her lip quivered and her eyes glistened with unshed tears. The fact that she cared so much about him made his heart lighter, even if she wouldn't say the words he needed.

"I swear if you get hurt again," she finally said, "I will leave you to rot where you fall." Her eyes narrowed when he burst into laughter. "Don't tempt me to hurt you myself."

"God, you're adorable," he stated just before he kissed her. As soon as this was over, he would tell her how he felt; how much she had changed his life and they could talk about the future.

They arrived at the Gold Pelican at the height of the lunch crowd. Cheyenne watched as Jake made a production of loudly greeting Cam and everyone else he knew before finding a stool at the bar for her. He hooked a foot on the rail and stood beside her.

"Couple of beers, Cam," he said, casually looking around while the bartender got their order. He turned back and nuzzled her ear as though in affection, yet his words were anything but loveable. "The sheriff is in a bright floral shirt and sunglasses near the front door," he whispered. "His deputy is the guy toward the back with a camera around his neck and geek glasses."

Cheyenne felt a little better knowing law enforcement was nearby, until Cam came back with their beers.

"Don't look now, but I think your two suspects have arrived. Mutt and Jeff and casually dressed like *Men in Black*?"

Jake nodded but acted nonchalant as he took a sip of beer and grabbed a handful of nuts from a nearby bowl. Cheyenne knew she would throw up if she drank her beer, so attempted a fake sip and the mere smell nearly did her in.

"I want this to be over," she hissed between clinched teeth. Jake put a hand on her back, rubbed, then let it slide up to squeeze her neck in a caress. "We know they're here; can't the sheriff arrest them now?"

185

"They haven't done anything," Jake replied. "Unless you want to start another fight, this time with them…" He grinned when she elbowed him in the ribs.

"Please don't," Cam said in passing. "I just got the last mess straightened out." He looked directly at Jake. "The bill's in the mail."

Jake downed the rest of his beer and took hers. "Got you covered," he said.

Cheyenne turned toward him. "That was not your fault. That man, Johnny Blaine, should be paying for it."

Cam snorted. "Ha. Getting money out of him would be like going fishing for Moby Dick." Under his breath, he added, "Mutt and Jeff have settled at a table by the piano. I'd say the next move is yours."

Jake moved away from the bar. "Darling, excuse me a minute."

Cheyenne didn't have time to savor his endearment. She grabbed his arm to stall him, but he simply gave her hand a squeeze and turned away. Her stomach dropped as she watched him saunter towards the restrooms at the back of the bar. She held her breath, watching for the two men to make a move. Several minutes passed and nothing happened. She turned back to thank Cam for the lemonade he had placed in front of her.

"Shit, not again." The words had barely left his mouth when Cheyenne heard a crash and several curses.

She swiveled to see the two men standing by an overturned table, shouting at some other nearby people. Those men in turn started swinging and a brawl erupted. She saw the deputy wade into the throng, then the sheriff rushed past her.

"Do something!" she cried at Cam.

"I think they have it in hand," he replied, nodding toward the back.

Cheyenne scanned the subdued crowd looking for Jake but she couldn't spot him. The sheriff and deputy were lining people up against the wall, shouting to be heard over the claims of who started the fight.

"Oh, dear god!" She reached across the bar to grab Cam's sleeve. "Those men are gone and I don't see Jake!"

"Sonofabitch." Cam rushed to the end of the bar, shouted for the sheriff and disappeared down the hall.

Cheyenne followed, determined to breach the men's restroom if necessary to find Jake. She was half way down the hall when Cam emerged from the men's room and rushed toward the back exit. He slammed open the emergency door and took a step into the alley, Cheyenne nearly running into his back as he stopped and looked both ways.

The alley was empty.

"Damn him! I told him this wouldn't work," she cried as she punched the bartender in the arm with her fist.

He didn't bother commenting as he turned her around and pushed her back inside. They hurried down the hall and into the bar, which was strangely quiet. When the sheriff spied them, he rushed over.

"Where's Jake?"

"They took him!" Cheyenne was in tears as she sank onto a nearby chair. Why had she not put her foot down? Why had Jake taken such a chance?

The sheriff was on the phone, his deputy on another one. When he finished, he finally spoke to her. "I called the ferry port and they'll make sure those two don't get on the ferry."

The deputy piped up. "McNally is down at the marina and he's got some others watching the boat slips."

Cam was righting the table and chairs and one of the waitresses was sweeping up broken glass and beer bottles. The sheriff went back to questioning the few men still lined up against the wall. No one seemed too concerned that Jake was missing.

"We have to do something!" she wailed to no one in particular and everyone in general.

"Nobody will get him off the island without our knowing it," the sheriff told her. "In fact, there's not much chance they can hide him without our finding out pretty damn quick."

"How can you be so casual? What if they hurt him?"

"Chances are," Cam told her, "they took him for ransom so they're not about to hurt him."

"Well that makes me feel so much better." Cheyenne stormed past him toward the front door.

"Where are you going? Jake asked me to keep an eye on you if things went sideways."

She spun around, hands on hips. "You are not my keeper. *Jake* is not my keeper. If none of you," she swung her arm wide to encompass the entire room, "are going to look for him, I will *do it myself.*" Her grand exit was spoiled as she turned and slammed into a body rushing into the bar.

"Sheriff, there's a ruckus down at the marina," Lindsay shouted as she threw her arms out to steady Cheyenne. "Come on." She grabbed Cheyenne's hand and they ran out of the bar. When Cheyenne headed toward the rickshaw, Lindsay tugged her the opposite way. "It's quicker to run."

Cheyenne felt she was in good shape but Lindsay quickly outdistanced her, as did the sheriff, deputy and Cam. She followed as fast as she could, weaving through pedestrians. They veered into the marina and down the docks to the left, finally coming to a halt by a slip housing a speed boat. If she hadn't been in fear for Jake's life, the scene that met them might have been funny.

One of the men in black was treading water off the end of the boat. Johnny Blaine held the shorter one by the ankles upside-down over the side of the boat, periodically dunking him under and pulling him back up sputtering. Jake lay in an unconscious heap on the dock. She rushed to his side while Cam and the deputy fished one man out of the water and the sheriff tried to convince Johnny to release the man he held.

"They were taking Jake away," Johnny stated calmly as he dunked the man again. "Said Jake was drunk and they were taking him back to the mainland. He don't belong on the mainland." Johnny looked at Cheyenne. "I know he don't drink like I do and I'm real sorry, Miss, for the trouble I caused you that other time." He seemed to have forgotten about the man he was holding under until his jerking and splashing caught his attention. This time, he yanked him up and dropped him in a heap on the deck of the boat. The sheriff had to wait until he quit coughing up water before he could handcuff him and get him onto the dock.

Jake moaned and Cheyenne quickly turned back to him. A bright purple bruise was already forming on his chin and when he opened his eyes, they didn't appear quite focused.

"Are you all right?"

"Hell, no." He tried to sit up and groaned. Cheyenne scooted around so she could cradle his head in her lap. She brushed the hair out of his eyes with one hand as the other lay across his chest.

In the hurry to get to the marina, no one had bothered with a vehicle, so it was some minutes later when the deputy was dispatched for the police car and Lindsay went back for her bike. The sheriff told Cheyenne to take care of Jake and he would call when he figured out what the two men were after. Lindsay helped Cheyenne get Jake into the rickshaw.

"We need to take you to Dr. Stephens," she said as he groaned upon sitting.

"Just get me back to the jeep and home," he replied, his voice so weak and low she had a hard time hearing. He limply lifted both hands, wiggling his fingers. "See, they still work."

At that point, Cheyenne completely lost it. "You idiot. You certifiable numbskull!" She stood by the rickshaw and ranted, uncaring of the crowd gathering as drenched men were hauled off in handcuffs, the blue and red lights of the sheriff's car blinking in the growing darkness.

"Do you think that's all I care about? I swear; I told you—"

He reached out and grabbed her wrist, pulling her against the side of the rickshaw. His other hand cupped the back of her neck and his mouth slammed against hers, effectively interrupting her tirade. He only softened the kiss

189

when she quit struggling, and he didn't let her go until cheering erupted.

"Get in," he said softly.

Cheeks hot with embarrassment as the crowd applauded, she squeezed in beside him and Lindsay pedaled them back to the Gold Pelican. Jake held his side as he climbed down and Cheyenne simply shook her head.

"Give me the keys," she said and was surprised when he complied without complaint. She helped him into the jeep and hurried around to the other side. It had been years since she'd driven a stick shift and he snorted when she popped the clutch and stalled. And then he was cradling her against his chest as huge sobs raked her. As strong as she had always thought herself, she was a complete mess when it came to him.

"I was so frightened," she sobbed, then hiccupped.

"It's all right, Cat. Everything is all right." He rubbed her back and kissed the top of her head.

"Nothing is all right," she blubbered. "You've been hurt twice since I've been here. People are trying to kidnap you. You said yourself you hadn't had any trouble before I came. It's all my fault."

Jake stiffened, not sure how to respond. Eventually someone would have recognized him and tried to make a fast buck. He didn't blame her for that. What was she saying; that she didn't want to be with him?

She pushed away and inadvertently hit his ribs. He couldn't stifle the groan.

"Oh, here you are hurt and I'm carrying on like it was me." She looked him over, caressing his cheek with her palm.

"Nothing is broken. Let's just go home."

This time he kept his mouth shut when she popped the clutch and they started to jerk along the street.

The bumping along the dirt road jarred him awake as Cheyenne pulled up beside the cottage. He tried to get out but his legs felt like lead. When she rushed over to his side, he let her help him into the house. His vision wavered and his legs gave out as they approached the bed. If it had been

190

any further away, he would have ended up on the floor. As it was, Cheyenne had to lift his legs onto the bed and remove his shoes.

"You should have let us take you to the doctor," she muttered, pushing to get him centered. "Why do you have to be so stubborn about everything?"

As before, he instinctively knew she was talking about more than the recent incident, but his brain couldn't process a coherent thought.

"Stay with me," he groped for her hand but she faded from view as darkness crept over him.

His dreams were intense; waves cresting over the side of a boat to which he clung, adrift on a raging sea. Everywhere he looked, dark water heaved beneath him and black clouds roiled above him. Suddenly vibrant colors flashed across the sinister sky and the voice of an angel beckoned him. Her voice was soothing, like music drifting on a breeze and he quit fighting the inevitable and sank into oblivion beneath the waves.

When Jake woke, morning sun streamed through the open window. Whatever those two had done to him, besides hitting him on the jaw, had left him with a blinding headache and he closed his eyes against the light. Snippets of a dream to which he couldn't recall details gave him an uneasy feeling; as though something were wrong but he couldn't put a finger on it. Panicking, he swung his feet off the bed and stood, swaying and grabbing the headboard.

And then he heard it; her voice from the other room. He breathed a sigh of relief to know she was still there. He stumbled to the bathroom for aspirin, splashed water on his face and walked into the living room as she was closing the front door.

"Coming...or going?" he asked and watched as she spun around in surprise. A guilty look quickly crossed her features and then was gone. He suddenly remembered his dream and the panic he had felt knowing she wasn't with him. Had his dream been a portent of the future?

Don't be an ass and push her, he told himself.

"Sorry." He brushed his hands through his hair. "Abominable headache."

"You should have gone..." she broke off. "Never mind. Come have some breakfast."

She turned to the small kitchen and he watched as she took a sheet of biscuits out of the oven. Piling them on a plate, she set them on the table with butter, poured two cups of coffee and joined him.

His phone rang and, seeing it was the sheriff, he put it on speaker.

"How you feeling, kid?"

"I've had better days, Sheriff. Please tell me you still have those two in custody."

"Actually, I don't; the Seattle police do." The sheriff laughed. "Seems they were ex-paparazzi who decided kidnapping could be more lucrative than taking photos. Once I posted mug shots, I got a call from LA saying they were wanted down there for attempting the same thing. The Seattle police will see that they get to LA."

"Attempting?" Jake asked.

"Yeah. It didn't work any better in LA than it did here, but they got away down there before the police could nab them."

"Well, that's kudos to you then."

"Reckon so," the sheriff said. "Later."

Jake punched disconnect and closed his eyes with a sigh. At least that was over.

"How *do* you feel?" Cheyenne asked, scrutinizing his face. She reached over to lightly touch the bruise on his jaw he had seen in the mirror.

"Like I got hit by a truck."

She pursed her lips and didn't respond.

"You're not going to say *I told you so?*"

"Apparently I don't need to." She stuck her tongue out at him and it made him laugh, which in turn made his head worse. He groaned.

"You shouldn't be out of bed." She shook her head.

"Then come back to bed with me." Not giving her time to protest, he took her hand and led her to the bedroom. He

192

pulled her down with him and stretched out, content to simply hold her. She laid her head on his chest and draped a leg over his, giving a huge sigh.

"What happens the next time, Jake?" she asked quietly.

He wrapped his arm around her shoulders. "I'm just a flash in the pan. By next week, some other celebrity will cause a ruckus and people will forget all about me. We can go back to our quiet existence."

He felt her stiffen and silently cursed. Even though neither had said the words, a clock ticked loudly in the small haven they had created. He knew what needed to be said.

"Stay with me, Cat." He caressed her back.

She lifted her head and he sealed her lips with his before she could say a word. He poured all his passion and love into the kiss and for a moment she didn't respond. When she did, it wasn't what he expected.

She tore her mouth from his, pushing against him to quickly roll off the bed.

"It's unfair of you to ask me that." Her words were angry; her stance stiff.

"Why; because you have to get back to Chicago? What do you owe my uncle?" He slid from the bed to stand directly in front of her.

"He gave me a job to do; you knew that from the beginning."

"Ah, yes. Bring the wayward nephew home, no matter what it takes."

The crack of her hand against his cheek echoed in the small room. The sting of it didn't hurt nearly as bad as the hurt he saw in her gaze.

"Cat." He held out a hand but she stepped back against the wall, her eyes full of regret, which only made him feel worse.

"Don't call me that. Get out."

In other circumstances he might have laughed, considering the cottage was his. But in his frustration he had lashed out and implied something he knew was wrong. Now, the best thing he could do was give her space to calm down; then they could talk. He slipped on his shoes and walked out the door.

He walked clear to the Ranger station, only to have Trevor tell him he was a fool and he'd better get things straightened out before it was too late.

Everything bounced and reverberated around in his brain all the way back to the cottage. He loved Cheyenne to distraction but had treated her poorly. This whole thing didn't really have to do with her at all; she was simply the messenger. His anger and aggravation should be directed solely at his uncle and it was up to Jake to make it right; not Cheyenne. He broke into a trot, anxious now to get back and tell her how much he loved her; that he would do whatever was necessary to earn her love. He could only pray she would forgive him.

"Cheyenne?" he called the moment he opened the door. Silence greeted him and he knew in a heartbeat that he was too late.

Chapter 18

Chicago, Illinois

Cheyenne stared at her computer screen, the screensaver showing myriad shades of red and orange across the sky; the setting sun over the bay only a sliver on the horizon. It was a photo she had taken at the cottage on Lockabee Island. Most days she wondered why she kept punishing herself with it.

It had been three weeks since her return. Her report to Sebastian Donovan had been short and curt. "He's on Lockabee Island off the coast of Washington. He doesn't want to come home." She had seen the disappointment on the man's face before he could hide it. There wasn't much the senior Donovan could hide these days. He was bedridden with a twenty-four hour nurse; never left his chambers in the mansion and didn't deal with the business aspects of the Academy at all. Everyone on the staff, including her, knew it was only a matter of time before the doors would close and they would be out of jobs.

It was more personal for her, however. She carried tremendous guilt for not having told Jake that his uncle was ill. Her stubborn pride and so called professionalism had caused her to do what she thought was right. Since her return, she had reached for the phone countless times yet never completed the call.

And therein lay her heartbreak. She knew if she heard his voice, she would completely come apart. As it was she wasn't sleeping. She would sit curled up on her couch, wrapped in Jake's old bass tee-shirt which she had stolen that last day, scrolling through photos of the town, the people, but especially of Jake. She paused at a photo of Lindsay. When Cheyenne had called that last day, Lindsay had gotten to the cottage almost before Cheyenne finished packing. She made the girl swear not to tell anyone where she had gone, but Cheyenne held little hope that she would keep that promise. After all, *it was Lockabee.* She made it just in time for the ferry and upon reaching the mainland reclaimed her car and drove clear to Seattle before stopping.

She kept wondering why she had left in anger instead of waiting for him to return. Why hadn't she told him she loved him and would stay if he simply went to Chicago to see his uncle?

But she knew it couldn't be an "I'll do this if you do that" scenario. Yet because of her commitment to his uncle, she hadn't been able to think of any other way out of her predicament.

She stood and walked to the window overlooking the back garden. Her heels clicked on the hardwood floors and her silk suit rustled softly against her hips. She had thought getting back to her job and donning the persona of Miss Tucker, she could forget. Instead, it only made her long for capris and flip-flops; sunglasses and her mermaid ball cap.

A commotion outside her office had her looking toward the door as it swung open, a yelp preceding the appearance of the receptionist on the heels of a dog trailing a leash.

"I'm so sorry, Miss Tucker. Mr. Donovan told me to bring him back to you but he got away from me."

The puppy, which she realized was her favorite from Trevor's litter, had skidded to a halt in front of Cheyenne and she squatted down to pet him. "What a sweetheart you are." She buried her face in the dog's soft fur, remembering. "Melissa, how on earth would Mr. Donovan have gotten this dog?"

"Perhaps you're thinking of the wrong Mr. Donovan." The masculine voice, seductively soft, caused her head to jerk up, her gaze colliding with dark chocolate eyes.

She practically fell off her high heels. Gathering the puppy in her arms, she slowly stood, her gaze never leaving his.

"I call him Fish Bait," he said.

"What a horrid name."

He took a step toward her. "Not when I want to lure a mermaid."

Her heart pounded at his words and she practically dropped the wiggling puppy. She wobbled a step to keep her balance.

"Nice shoes," he said, glancing down at her new red strappy heels.

"Thank you for buying them for me."

"I didn't..." he started with a frown, then burst out laughing. "God, I've missed your smart mouth, Miss Tucker."

Suddenly she was engulfed in his embrace. He was warm as the summer sun and he smelled like the ocean breeze. He pulled the puppy from her grasp, hooking it under one arm as the other came around her and his mouth descended to hers. His kiss was lightning and shooting stars and bottle rockets. She wrapped her arms around his neck and simply held on, letting him carry her away. She had no idea where the kiss might have led if not for wet seeping through her skirt and running down her leg.

"Oh, no," she moaned as Jake released her and set the puppy on the floor.

"Is that any way to treat a lady, you mongrel?" He tried to sternly reprimand the pup but she could hear laughter in his voice.

"Jake Smith, I swear! I can't believe in less than five minutes you ruined yet another suit."

"It wasn't my fault," he replied as he stood and then it was Cheyenne's turn to laugh. A wet spot spread across the side of his polo shirt and ran down the leg of his khaki slacks. "He's just happy to see you."

She looked up to find his gaze intent on her. "I'm very happy to see you, too." And magically her world righted again.

Jake cleared his throat. "I came to give my uncle what he wants."

"Have you seen him?" she asked.

He shook his head. "He wasn't my first priority."

"You could have come with me," she said softly.

Again he shook his head. "The puppy needed shots before transport and," he paused, looking off to the side, "there was business to finish."

Cheyenne realized the puppy had nothing to do with it. Jake had waited past the deadline to return so that he could *win*. Yet he had come home, so in truth his uncle had also won. And then it dawned on her what he really meant.

"You finished it?"

He nodded.

"But the deadline for the Camelot Awards was last week."

"It was in the mail by then." His gaze found hers and all she could do was smile.

"What did you title it?"

"A Mermaid's Tears."

She immediately shook her head. "That doesn't sound inspiring. You have no sense of style." She waved toward the puppy. "Just look what you named that adorable puppy."

He slowly walked toward her until they were toe to toe. He cradled her face in his hands; those long slender fingers sliding into her hair and shaking it loose from her clip. His kiss was as light as butterfly wings, yet it singed her clear to her toes.

"I love you, Cheyenne Alyce Tucker. If I titled it *Tales of a Mermaid*, would it have a happy ending?"

She could feel tears slipping from beneath her lashes. "If you tell me again that you love me."

He did, and she knew the mermaid would live happily ever after.

* * *

The winner of the Camelot Award for Excellence in Musical Composition was announced the next week. Jake was at his uncle's bedside as the old man read the letter from the committee. He didn't show much reaction, but then he hadn't spoken in months and could barely lift his head from his pillow. The letter dropped to the coverlet but when Jake reached for it, his uncle covered the single sheet with his bony hand, fingers shaking as he blindly felt for the embossed seal of the Camelot Institute. His other hand shook as he raised it and Jake clasped it in both of his.

He looked up, found his uncle's watery gaze and gave him his best smile. His uncle's eyes closed and the air stilled around them. Tears fell as he gently laid his uncle's lifeless hand on his chest, picked up the letter and walked out of the room. Cheyenne would probably want to frame it and glancing down, he had to admit he wasn't disappointed.

Dear Misters Donovan,

It is with pleasure that the Camelot Institute is offering the Camelot Award to "Tales of a Mermaid", composed by Sebastian and Joseph Donovan.

The demo CD submitted by Michael Gilbert of the Los Angeles Symphony left the committee breathless and in awe of the genius combination of melodies that created this true work of art. Mr. Gilbert's nomination letter leads us to believe that without Sebastian Donovan's exceptional assiduousness and Joseph Donovan's incredible gift, this composition might never have been born. That would, indeed, have been a tragic loss for the musical world.

Congratulations.

Epilogue

It was the third year for the Donovan Music Camp and as usual the place was busy. Cheyenne wandered from the office through the kitchen, grabbing a fresh baked chocolate chip cookie from the tray Brenda Kay had just pulled from the oven.

"Watch yourself. Those are hot," she said. Eyeing Cheyenne's nonexistent waist, she added, "Are you even supposed to be eating chocolate?"

"The nice thing about being pregnant is I can eat whatever I please. The problem will come after the birth when I have to get rid of the extra pounds. Do you know where Jake is?"

Brenda Kay had handed her restaurant in town over to her daughter and son-in-law and now ran the kitchen at the camp where they served three meals a day to growing eight to fifteen year olds. The only stipulation Cheyenne had made at the time Jake hired her was that whatever she fixed for meals, silverware was required. Now, she absently waved a hand, which meant Jake could be anywhere on the three acre compound.

The clicking sound of Fish Bait's toe nails echoed her flip-flops as they walked across the cavernous cafeteria, the gleaming tiles and newly painted walls awash in morning light from the skylights above. To her right was the dormitory that housed the boys and girls for a month at a time as they attended camp. To the left of the cafeteria, which also served as performance hall, were a row of individual, state of the art practice cubicles.

Jake had purchased the small cottage and surrounding land upon their return to Lockabee after their honeymoon. Construction on the facilities had started immediately and the first camp had followed the next summer.

She slipped on her sunglasses as she exited the building; or actually Jake's glasses as she was constantly losing hers and she rather liked wearing his aviator style mirrored shades. She absently patted the big dog's head as she looked about for her husband. Even though Jake had originally brought the dog to Chicago, he had always been Cheyenne's dog. He was extremely protective; especially now when she was pregnant, sometimes even growling at Jake.

Off to the south past the cottage she heard hollering as the afternoon swim lessons were in full force, but she turned the opposite way, having an intuitive feel for where her husband might be. She rounded the corner of the main building, looking past the basketball courts and sand volleyball pit to the baseball field.

It might look like an ordinary camp, if one didn't know Jake's background. While some of the children who attended had exceptional musical talent, the camp was open to anyone. And though music took up a large portion of the campers' day, there was always time for swimming and sports; all the types of activities Jake had missed out on as a youngster. There were fishing excursions, campfires and hikes through the woods.

Through word of mouth alone, the camp was often host to world renowned musical celebrities, all wanting to help instill a love of music in the youngsters who attended. Many of those same celebrities gave very generous donations to the camp because no one paid tuition. Travel scholarships were readily available to any impoverished child who wrote Jake a simple request. And that was exactly why she needed to speak to him.

She found him at home plate, patiently giving instructions to the batter, who swung too low; the bat slipping out of his little hands and flying straight at Jake's shin. Cheyenne winced as he hopped in a circle, then seeing her, slowly hobbled over to where she stood, safely behind the fence.

"Why the face?" he asked, as if he didn't know. It wasn't that long ago that he had ended up at Doctor Stephen's with a twisted ankle after a free-for-all basketball game with a bunch of campers. The man refused to grow up.

"I do not need you to be a patient in the hospital at the same time I am," she said, rubbing her belly.

He circled her waist, pulling her back against his chest and tapping his fingers across her abdomen like he was playing a piano keyboard. The baby returned his attention with a healthy kick, making him laugh.

"What else?" he asked at her sigh.

She held up the ledger sheets but knew if it wasn't a musical score, Jake could care less. "We're still losing money."

He kissed the side of her neck and a shiver raced down her spine. He could still make a mess of her with a simple kiss.

"Are we destitute?"

"Well, of course not, but…"

His breath tickled her ear. "Then it's all good, mermaid." The baby kicked against his hand again. "In fact, it's absolutely perfect."

The End

Also by Barbara Baldwin

Spinning Through Time
A Game of Love
Always Believe
Prospecting for Love
If Wishes Were Magic
Tenderhearted Cowboy
Love in Disguise
An Interlude
Before Tomorrow Comes
Hold On To The Past
Prelude and Promises

Barbara resides in the Midwest but she loves to travel and explore new places, which usually means each of her novels is set in a different locale. She has been published in formats from poetry and short stories to full-length fiction. She really loves writing romance, whether it is contemporary, historical or time travel. She has an MA in Communication and has taught every grade from Kindergarten to college. Visit her website at http://www.authorsden.com/barbarajbaldwin.

www.ingramcontent.com/pod-product-compliance
Lightning Source LLC
Chambersburg PA
CBHW020647260626
47157CB00008B/2941

* 9 7 8 0 2 2 8 6 0 5 6 2 1 *